# *What You Cannot Tell*

Praise for *Sabbath Creek*:

"...a transcendent coming-of-age story that feels unshackled to any place and time. Its sense of place, however, is pungently particular, infused with the surface languor and latent violence of the Deep South...This spare, lovely novel, while generous in humor, is anchored by sorrow and interspersed with portents of tragedy."

—*The New York Times Book Review*

Praise for *The Sweet Everlasting*:

"*The Sweet Everlasting* is one of the best books of fiction I have ever read. From beneath an iron-tough exterior emerges a durable tenderness as clear as any sunrise. How Judson Mitcham has done it, I can't say, but his first novel is a masterpiece."

—Fred Chappell

## *Also by Judson Mitcham*

NOVELS
*The Sweet Everlasting*
*Sabbath Creek*

POETRY
*Somewhere in Ecclesiastes*
*This April Day*
*A Little Salvation*

ANTHOLOGY
*Inspired Georgia*

CHAPBOOK
*Notes for a Prayer in June*

# *What You Cannot Tell*

*a novel*

---

Judson Mitcham

---

Mercer University Press
Macon, Georgia

MUP/ P733


Published by Mercer University Press
1501 Mercer University Drive
Macon, Georgia 31207



30 29 28 27 26 5 4 3 2 1

Books published by Mercer University Press are printed on acid-free paper that meets the requirements of the American National Standard for Information Sciences—Permanence of Paper for Printed Library Materials.

Printed and bound in the United States.

This book is set in Adobe Caslon

Cover/jacket design by Burt&Burt.

Cataloging-in-Publication Data is available from the Library of Congress
Names: Mitcham, Judson author
Title: What you cannot tell : a novel / Judson Mitcham.
Description: Macon, Georgia : Mercer Univesity Press, 2026. | Summary: "What You Cannot Tell employs a first-person narrator, who takes a job teaching psychology at a historically black college in 1974, at the age of twenty-six"—Provided by publisher.
Identifiers: LCCN 2025038178 (print) | LCCN 2025038179 (ebook) |
ISBN 9798897360079 paperback | ISBN 9798897360086 ebook
Subjects: LCGFT: Fiction | Novels
Classification: LCC PS3563.I7356 W47 2026 (print) | LCC PS3563.I7356 (ebook)
LC record available at https://lccn.loc.gov/2025038178
LC ebook record available at https://lccn.loc.gov/2025038179

*In memory of Glenn Hawkins, Jr.*

MERCER UNIVERSITY PRESS

*Endowed by*

TOM WATSON BROWN

*and*

THE WATSON-BROWN FOUNDATION, INC.

*What You Cannot Tell*

# PART ONE

*Truth is what you cannot tell...*
*Truth is the trick that History,*
*Over and over again, plays on us...*
*Truth is the Serpent's joke*

*—Robert Penn Warren*

## *1. October, 2002*

The college let me go last May, after twenty-eight years. They had cause. This happened the same week I found out I was very sick, but nobody knew about that, and only a few people know about it now.

After the doctor had spoken with me, I went into the restroom and threw up and stayed on my knees. When I stood and looked in the mirror, a ghostly white face drained of blood stared me down. I walked out on weak legs, queasy and hot all over, a solitary and terrified witness to my own life. I tried to take control of the news, to treat it like a number I could slip into my wallet and forget.

I stepped out of the elevator onto the fifth level of the parking deck. A battered car rattled past, its windows so dark it had no driver, a ruined machine clanking its way out into the world with no one to guide it, the smell of gasoline washing along with the exhaust. I heard it descend, heard the tires wail and echo.

And all day today, I've thought about Claude and Arlene Jackson, how long they've been gone now, and how much they must have loved each other.

## *2.*

I'm living in Monroe, where I grew up—an hour east of Atlanta, four hours north of the college. My brother Donnie and his wife, Charlotte, have a large old house and they wanted me to move in there, but I'm living in an extended-stay motel. I've stored some boxes in Donnie's garage, mostly papers and books I packed up when I left the college. He'll have to decide what to do with it all, so when I feel able, I grab a box and bring it back to the motel and take a look. Nearly everything goes into garbage bags.

*3.*

A page of instructions for producing an "apparitional experience." I once tried it on myself, wondering if maybe I could use it in class, which makes no sense to me now ("Strange-face-in-the-mirror illusion" from the journal *Perception*).

> "Set out two chairs about two feet apart in a dimly lit room. Place a large mirror on one chair and have the person sit on the other chair so that they can stare at their reflection in the near darkness. After people look at their reflection for about a minute, they may see unsettling changes. The eyes may start to move or shine, the mouth open, the nose grow very large. Eventually, completely new faces may appear—human or animal, living or dead, and some may be monstrous. Strong emotional responses often accompany these perceptions. Some people feel threatened by the face in the mirror."

I dimmed the lights and set up the chairs and the mirror and stared at myself for a while. Nothing happened. I tried again a week or so later. I thought maybe the room hadn't been dark enough. I made that change, and I sat there and doubted anything would happen.

But then my eyes dissolved and hollowed out into skull holes, my mouth jacked itself open, my tongue flared out into the fanged spade-head of a snake and struck at my face.

I lurched away and escaped, and when I looked in the mirror again, all I saw was my own dim self.

But the snake was real, and still in the room, and if I arranged a few things correctly, it would come back. Even now, wherever I go, I know it's with me.

*4.*

The newspaper box at the motel is empty. I walk across the street to the Circle K. As I leave the store, a young woman materializes from behind the gas pumps and asks if I can spare a few dollars for gas.

She's maybe thirty-five, wearing jeans and a T-shirt. Her blonde hair is pulled back into a short ponytail, under a Florida Gators cap. She tells me her husband just put a gun to her head, and my first impulse is to ask, "Was it the cap?" but there are limits to playing the fool.

She says, "I packed some things and got in the car. You can see my stuff there. I don't have any money. He put a hold on the ATM. Can you please help me? I'll take anything."

She's driving a Honda SUV, not very old. I see a suitcase and a box and a laundry basket full of clothes. A Walton County tag. In God We Trust. It's a good strategy for a scam. Pack the car and look for suckers. Be on God's side.

"Please," she says. "*Please* help me."

"How do I know you're telling me the truth?"

"I guess you don't, but it *is* the truth. I swear to God."

I give her fourteen dollars, which is what I have on me, and I cross the road and head for the motel, heavy with that old familiar feeling—I wish I knew what to believe.

*5.*

Notes I can't identify, in my handwriting. I have no memory of this, don't know the source.

-two people talking
-they understand each other and fall silent
-a long silence, the silence is language
-man is not in time, like a body immersed in a river
-time is <u>in</u> him
-a historical creature but a creature of solitude
-the awareness that men die
-the awareness that <u>I</u> am going to die
-these are separate awarenesses

*6.*

Donnie and Charlotte are outside with their two-year-old granddaughter, Iris, who's staying with them now. Elizabeth, their only child, has left her daughter here while she deals with problems at home in Nashville.

Iris rides a Big Wheel in and out of the carport. She can't reach the pedals, and scoots along by shoving off with her feet.

The last time I visited, I watched them take turns pushing her up the driveway's gradual slope, where they'd release her and she'd glide down into the carport. They're sitting in lawn chairs, watching her ride in a circle. They look tired. I take a chair off the carport wall and have a seat. Iris bumps the Big Wheel into Donnie's leg.

"Push the hill, Pa," she says. Donnie repositions the Big Wheel.

"Uncle Everett wants to push you now, sweetie."

"No, Pa, you."

"Well, but how about Uncle Everett? Look, Iris, this is my baby brother."

I ask if I can push her up the hill just one time. I'm not sure I can.

"*Never,*" she says. Donnie and Charlotte burst out laughing.

Iris walks the Big Wheel out of reach with fast little choppy steps and gives me a pouty face. Charlotte explains that the no typical of two-year-olds has recently become a never for Iris.

"Last night, when I said it was time for her to take a bath, she said, 'Never.' For the last week, she's kept us laughing. Never to everything. More cereal? Never. Let's get your shoes on. Never."

Donnie pushes the child up the hill and she squeals her way to the bottom and wants more. He sits and rests for a minute, and then they start up the hill again.

Charlotte says it looks like we might get some rain. "Dry as a bone all last month, but for the last little while it has rained a right smart, as my mama used to say."

Bruised clouds scud over the pines, the wind lifts Donnie's hair, and a few long strands hang over his left ear. He makes sure Iris is all set, he tells her to hold on tight, and he lets her go.

7.

Donnie and I were raised by our grandparents. Our grandfather passed away when I was eighteen, and I was in my third year of teaching when my grandmother underwent an operation she did not survive. On the morning of the surgery, I drove her to Emory Hospital, heading due west on Highway 78, the sun rising behind us and casting long shadows.

My grandmother was not a talkative person, but that morning she talked to me the whole way to the hospital. She'd taken the tranquilizer the doctor had given her for sleep, but said she hadn't slept. She talked about my mother as a little girl, about the baby doll she played with until it fell apart. When my grandmother tried to sew it back together, it couldn't be done, a failure that was still inside her, all these years later.

*8.*

When I first moved back to Monroe, I didn't want to tell Donnie and Charlotte all the details of my illness. I said the doctors didn't give me much time, and there was nothing to be done. Charlotte didn't understand why I wouldn't tell them exactly what was wrong with me. Donnie told her I had always been a stubborn jackass and that I was going to do exactly what I wanted to, and it didn't do anybody the least bit of good to get all worked up about it.

Charlotte said they only wanted to support me and to help me. She said, "If it's cancer, Everett…" When she started to cry, I was surprised by how distraught she was, and I went ahead and told them, with the understanding that after I did, they wouldn't try to make me talk about it.

I have a large benign growth between the cerebellum and the occipital lobes. It can't be treated surgically. It's called a falco-tentorial meningioma. To operate would be unwise because of the depth and the size of the growth and because of the surrounding deep cerebral veins. It's causing compression of the midbrain and will eventually cause respiratory failure. The doctors discuss strategies of palliative care. Most of the time, there's little evidence I'm not well. But some days, I wake up and everything has gone sideways, and when I move, I feel so sick that all I want is for it to be over.

*9.*

A deep blue day, early afternoon. I take a left onto the smooth blacktop and head for Donnie's house, four miles down this road that once cut through cotton fields but now curves through subdivisions and past a golf course, though it's not exactly the same road, having been diverted eastward for maybe a hundred yards and then returned to its old path.

Out on the golf course a lake flares tarnished light and disappears. The entrance to the course is blocked by fences thick with vines, a tall wrought-iron gate next to a brick guard station, a man visible in the doorway.

Nobody comes to the front door at Donnie's house. I could go on in, but I don't like to do that. I walk around to the back yard, and Charlotte steps onto the porch.

"I tried the front."

"Hey," she says. "I didn't hear you. Good Lord, Everett."

"Oh, I fell and hit my head, but I'm okay."

"Donnie's in the shower, and I was running the dishwasher. Come on in."

She gives me a hug and a kiss on the cheek, and we go inside. "The baby's taking a nap. That's a bad bruise."

"It looks worse than it is."

She touches my left temple. "Well, it looks pretty bad."

Donnie shuffles in. He's barefoot, wearing sweat pants and a T-shirt. His sparse hair is wet, with longs strands plastered across his scalp. He says, "How you making it, little brother? *Damn*, what happened to you?"

"Nothing. I mean, it's not bad. My knee gave out, and I fell and hit my head, but I'm all right."

"Did you get it looked at?"

"Well, *y'all* are looking at it right now."

"That's real good, smart ass."

"It looks worse than it is."

The kitchen smells like our home long ago—fried chicken and cabbage and cornbread and tomatoes cooked down. We watch Charlotte turning the chicken, then Donnie nods toward the main room, where the TV is. "Why don't we move in there?"

I'm at the end of the sofa, and he's in his recliner. On the coffee table, there are two stuffed animals, a bunny and a kitten. On the floor there's a toy barn surrounded by little plastic horses and cows and pigs and lions and tigers and giraffes and walruses and whales and elephants.

There's also a tractor, a dump truck, and a few matchbox cars. Those are the toys Donnie has bought for himself.

He picks up the remote and turns on the TV, tuned to ESPN. He puts it on mute, with closed captions, and we keep watching the screen—a compilation of bad plays: fielding errors, dropped passes, players tripping and whiffing and misjudging, running in the wrong direction.

He says, "You remember when Randy Johnson caught that bird with a fastball and killed it?"

"Is that what you brought me in here to talk about?"

"Bird comes out of nowhere, right into the pitch, then explodes. They've shown that a bunch of times lately. I guess it's been about a year since it happened, and I imagine that's why they're showing it. They slow it down, and you can see the bird flop over to the side and the ball roll toward the stands, and you can see the crowd start to realize what happened."

On the screen, a high school basketball player steals the ball from his own teammate, dribbles the length of the court, and scores for the other team. Donnie flips the channel to CNN, where they are reporting on a workplace shooting—four people dead, including the shooter. We watch for a while and he turns it off.

"You remember Ricky Hines? He was a grade ahead of me in school? Played tackle?"

A big redheaded boy with a crewcut and squinty eyes—that's all I remember.

"Shot his wife and his grown daughter and her little girl and shot himself. Shot the dogs too, I understand. Up in Illinois or Indiana or somewhere, about two years back. I only just heard about it. You'd think it would have been big news, but I guess not."

Charlotte calls us to the table. I take small helpings but can't really eat. She wants to know if there's anything else she can get me. I ask if she has buttermilk, and she pours me half a glass, and I crumble cornbread in it and top it off with black pepper, and I'm able to eat that. In fact, it's a treat.

We all move back into the TV room. Donnie starts to say something but then we can hear Iris crying. Charlotte gets up and brings her back and rocks her awhile, until Iris climbs down and picks up two plastic animals, a tiger and a giraffe, and starts a conversation between them.

*10.*

I applied to graduate school for no reason but to escape the draft. This was during the Vietnam War. Donnie got into the National Guard because he put his name on a waiting list, which I never did. When they created a new unit, he was in line to join. His unit was a refuge for the privileged—boys from wealthy families or with political or business or church connections—but most of the recruits were like Donnie, just white boys from the local area who had put their names on the list. So I applied to graduate school, hoping for a student deferment, but the draft board summoned me for a physical, and I was pretty sure I'd be drafted, but my left knee was bad enough to keep me out. And my admission to graduate school was a fluke. I scored okay on the GRE, and when a student dropped out at the last minute, they let me in on a provisional, with no financial aid. I was twice close to dismissal, but I did manage to get a master's degree. And because in those days the department had an overly generous policy allowing its own master's graduates to take some doctoral courses, without degree candidacy, I continued in school, which was not the best idea I ever had.

It had taken me almost six years to finish my undergraduate degree. I withdrew several times to make money, working mostly as a laborer on construction jobs. The whole time

I was in college I was employed as a night clerk at the Bulldog Inn in Athens.

Most nights there were uneventful. I sat behind the counter and studied but often slept. I developed a technique useful later on for sleeping in my office at the college. I'd prop my feet up and lean back and close my eyes, holding an open book face down on my chest. At the sound of the door, I would raise the book. The motel was robbed twice while I was on duty. A man came in at 3:38 AM—the police kept making me repeat the time—and pointed a pistol at me and told me to give him the money, which I did. When the man pointed his gun at me, I was afraid it would go off accidentally. I don't know why, but I didn't think he would really shoot me. It occurs to me now that maybe I had foolishly seen myself as part of some larger story that did not involve my getting shot.

The second robbery was only a month after the first. The investigating officers—one white and one black—suspected me of being a participant. They questioned me at length, and I thought they were going to charge me.

"Well, I guess you do know," I told them, "there's no way for me to prove the negative."

The white officer said, "You need to shut the fuck up."

They asked me to describe the man. I said he was a black man. What was he wearing? A shirt and pants and shoes. Young or old? Older. I told them he looked a little like Slappy White, the comedian. The black officer was writing down my statement. He stopped and looked up at the other policeman and then at me.

"Is that what you want me to put down here? He looked like Slappy White? Is that the best you can do?"

It was.

## *11.*

I'm in Winder getting a haircut, the only man in the salon. The women talk as if I'm not here, or so it seems. They talk about their plans for the weekend. Andrea, the woman cutting my hair, is headed to Tybee Island with her husband as soon as she gets off work. Someone is attending a wedding. She mentions the bride's name, and somebody else knows the groom's mother. Andrea doesn't know the couple. She shouts over the noise of a dryer, "What does he do?" The dryer stops whirring. The woman says, "He's a doctor at the medical college in Augusta. Carol said he does research on genetics. I don't really know."

Andrea steps back and tells the room she hopes he's not involved with that cloning thing she saw on TV, where they clone animals. "They'll be cloning people before you know it, and that's just not right."

The woman says, "It's some kind of genetic research, that's all I know. But I agree with you. Only God can make a life."

A voice says, "At least that's the way it *ought* to be."

A dryer starts up. Andrea parts my hair, combs it precisely and gently and smooths it with her hand. She has a loving touch. She leans close, and in a voice that only I can hear, she says, "I *would* like to see my mama and daddy again, though."

I'm walking to my car, thinking about a world in which Andrea's understanding is correct, in which cloned beings reappear fully formed, histories and personalities and souls intact, as if copied in all their dimensions and reanimated—a world wherein resurrection could occur—and I have to smile. But there was real heartache in her voice, and I wonder why she let me hear it, and only me, a stranger.

*12.*

Donnie calls and says he's coming over. He brings Iris with him. He's watching her all the time, ready to shield her or pick her up or take something from her hand.

"I called you right after breakfast," he says, "but you didn't answer."

"Yeah, I couldn't sleep. I got up early and drank some coffee and then went out for a drive. Out to the graveyard. I do that sometimes, you know. And then I drove to Winder and got a haircut."

"Why would you drive to Winder for a haircut?"

"I didn't drive to Winder for a haircut. I was driving around and ended up there and thought I'd get a haircut. There was a sign in the window. Is that all right with you?"

"I don't care *what* you do. I was only calling to check in with you. But look, why don't you have a cell phone like everybody else?"

"Now why would I want a cell phone? So I can be at the mercy of other people every goddamned minute of my life?"

"Fine by me. Do what you want. But with the way your health is, I mean, it wouldn't be a bad idea. You can turn it off, you know."

"I won't be getting a cell phone."

"Suit yourself."

We drive to the Dairy Queen, and we all have ice cream. Donnie and I take turns wiping the chocolate off Iris's hands and face, and when we're done, he goes back to the restroom and returns with wet paper towels to clean her up.

They bring me back to the motel, and he tells Iris to say goodbye but she shakes her head. After they've gone, I walk over to Denny's and sit in my usual booth, where I'm waited on by Juanita, an attractive woman only a few years younger. We're in the habit of modestly flirtatious exchanges.

Today she can see I'm not up to it. I ask her if she'll bring me a glass of ice water. When I go back to my room, it's dark and sour. I lie down to sleep and don't much care if I wake up or not.

*13.*

Notes on *Even the Rat Was White* by Robert Guthrie (1976)

-chapter headings:
-The Noble Savage and Science
-Brass Instruments and Dark Skins
-Psychometric Scientism
-Psychology and Race

Robert Guthrie: "One could dismiss the early anthropometric findings as quaint examples of misguided scientists during a period of widespread racism were it not for the fact that these views molded the psyches of many Americans in various mixtures of arrogance and fear."

From *The Black Man: The Comparative Anatomy and Psychology of the African Negro* by Hermann Burmeister (1853): "It is not worthwhile to look into the soul of the negro."

*14.*

At the yard sale after my grandmother died, people asked me where I was living and what I was doing. When I told them where I was teaching, I heard things like, "Well, I guess that's kind of interesting," or "I'll bet you got some stories to tell," both of which were true. One of the high school football coaches knew Wesley Banks, the long-time head coach who had left the college the year before I arrived. "Really one of the sharpest minds I've ever known," he said. "He really was. I'm sorry you missed him." And there was a woman high up in the Women's Missionary Union who picked through the costume jewelry at the yard sale and scowled and bought nothing, and who smiled at me sweetly and said, "Now Everett, I've been around them a long time, and there's one thing I know, and you know it too, if you're telling the truth. They can go to school and college and get all kinds of degrees and such, but they still can't pronounce their words right. I've never seen a one that could."

*15.*

I began teaching at the college in 1974. People from the small town had brought suit in federal court, demanding the college desegregate—and now a consent decree called for the hiring of more white faculty. I thought I would be there no more than a year or two.

Faculty housing was taken, and everywhere else was filled by students, so I found a mobile home for rent, a single-wide Shelby, furnished and air-conditioned. I had lived in a trailer before, and I was comfortable there.

The young woman one space over said she'd heard I taught at the black college—*black* was not the word she used—and she asked me if that was true. I said yes, it was. She said, "What's *that* like?"

I said, "Well, I don't really know yet. I was just glad to get the job."

"Shoot, I'd be scared. You not scared?"

I could have said, "I'd be scared if I went out there and used that *word*," but it was easier to say nothing, and easy was okay with me.

## *16.*

When I came to campus for my interview, I met with a search committee chaired by Dr. W. L. B. Reid, a tall man with close-cropped gray hair and heavy black horn-rim glasses and a bass voice so deep it verged on being a disability. He could stop a meeting by trying to whisper.

Dr. Reid's field was American History, and he was the longtime chair of the Social Sciences Division. The others were Mrs. Arlene Jackson, an art professor, and Dr. Clarence Plant, who would be my supervisor in the Psychology Department.

They had interviewed two other candidates, they said, but they had studied my credentials and had already chosen me. I was surprised and a little frightened. I had never thought I would actually *get* the job and have to do it. One of my professors had informed me of the job opportunity and strongly suggested I apply. He knew some people at the college.

The committee reviewed my course assignments for the quarter and gave me advice about how to make preparations. Then Dr. Reid told me the formal interview had ended, and since they'd already decided the job was mine, they wanted to go ahead and have a more personal conversation that was not to be considered part of the interview.

We would be discussing matters outside the scope of what could properly be raised in a job interview, he told me, and since I would likely be serving on committees like this one someday, he wanted to make sure that I understood correct procedure.

Arlene Jackson asked me about my family and my upbringing. I told them I had a brother named Donnie, three years older. We'd been raised by our maternal grandparents, Arlo and Edna Moon, who had given us their last name. Our father had left us when we were small—I have no memory of him—and our mother was emotionally unwell. For most of her adult life, she was in Central State Hospital in Milledgeville.

"Both my grandparents worked at a cotton mill in Monroe, where I grew up. Then I went to college at the University of Georgia in Athens."

Dr. Reid had been leaning back in his chair. He sat up straight and pulled a document from a folder and looked at it.

"Granddaddy was a loom-fixer and Grandma was a spinner. Those were good jobs in the mill, but they didn't make enough to help out with my college expenses, so I've borrowed a lot of money over the years, and I really need this job."

“Well, son,” Dr. Reid said, “we just told you that you have the job. So let’s talk about a few other matters.”

Dr. Plant asked if I thought my youth might be a factor in my working at the college, then asked me the same question about my race.

I said I was sure neither would be a problem. I told them I didn’t really think of myself as young—they found this amusing; I was twenty-six—and I offered a wise thought or two about race, which they accepted without comment or change of expression.

I did know enough not to call a black person by his or her first name unless they asked me to do so. I’d grown up under the rude etiquette of Jim Crow, where every black person was a Jimmy or a Susie, not a Mr. Smith or a Ms. Jones.

So at the college, I decided to address everyone formally, including students, unless they asked otherwise. Even then, I often stayed with the formality. It was a safe thing to do, and it was easy.

Dr. Plant said to call him whatever I chose. I would learn that he had an identical twin brother and was often called Twin by people who knew him well. Almost nobody called him Clarence. I addressed him as Dr. Plant. Arlene wished to be called Arlene, but Dr. Reid was always Dr. Reid. It would have seemed unnatural to call him Wallace Lee. In all the time I knew him, he never asked me to.

*17.*

When the interview was over, Dr. Plant took me to lunch at a place called Miss Mary’s, and later that afternoon we made the long drive out to Arlene Jackson’s house, where she and her husband, Claude, held a small gathering on most Fridays. People showed up around four to have a drink, but rarely did anyone drink a lot, since the Jacksons discouraged that.

They meant to enjoy those afternoons in their own way, and what they wanted was an occasion for people whose company they valued to relax in their home, have a drink or two if they chose, and talk at leisure about their ideas and their work—what they had observed or created or read.

There was to be no gossip, no campus politics, no complaining about students or administrators, nothing from what was called "the street committee." These were excluded, along with sports talk, as the usual and most natural topics, tending to preclude discussions of other things.

But the rules were always broken. Claude Jackson was the football team's biggest supporter, the president of its booster club, and if football came up, he couldn't let it go, and people found it hard to resist talking college politics.

At the Jacksons' that afternoon were Dr. Reid and his wife, Mabel, secretary to the college president; Wilma Caruthers, head of the English Department; Camille Williams, a striking young woman who worked in the library and was said to be the poet in residence; Artis Boone, an economist; Amin Mirza, an Iranian of the Bahá'í faith who taught physics; and Curtis Oliver, from the Music Department.

We all went into the sunroom of the house Arlene and Claude had built themselves, a locally famous structure, known for the murals Arlene painted on the south wall of the house and for the odd angularity of the building's asymmetrical design.

People helped themselves at the bar, but Arlene served me my drink. When we had all settled in, Mrs. Reid asked how the interview had gone. I told her I hoped it had gone well.

Dr. Plant said, "It did go well. Mr. Moon here seems to be a good fit for us, in several ways. He'll get that dissertation finished this year, and he'll be all set."

"Wonderful."

"The dissertation is not done?" Dr. Mirza's English was precise and formal, but his words were painful to hear. They scraped their way out of his throat, which was clearly damaged somehow. "It is hard to finish such a project while teaching. Am I wrong to say this?"

"No, Mirza, you're right, you are," Dr. Reid said. "But we think this young man will follow through. We have every confidence that he will."

"He's already made good progress," Dr. Plant said. "The research is done. He just has to write it up. Is that fair to say?"

"Yes, sir," I said. "Absolutely."

I told them I had gathered all the data—that was not true; I had gathered none—and that I still needed to run some statistical analyses, and then I'd start writing.

Dr. Mirza said, "So you have not *written* any of it?" He shook his head slowly. "There are many unfortunate stories I could tell you. Many of them. You must be very disciplined to do what you are trying to do."

"That's understating it," Dr. Caruthers said, "given the teaching load you'll have."

"Yes, ma'am," I said. "I know that's true. I've got a lot of hard work ahead of me."

Claude asked Dr. Reid if he'd had any time to devote to his project.

"Man, this accreditation committee? I'm telling you. I'm ready to be through with all that, but don't let me get started. As far as the project, though, I'm not where I need to be."

I asked him what his project was. It seemed like the right thing to do.

"Well," he said, and he laughed a little, "I call myself working on another book. This one might happen, it might not."

Dr. Plant told me about the psychology lecture series he was planning. He hoped to bring in Robert Guthrie, a friend of his who would soon be publishing a book called *Even the Rat Was White*. He asked me if I had heard of Dr. Guthrie's work. I had not.

Artis Boone asked Claude if he knew the status of the football team's star linebacker, who had run into eligibility problems. Arlene was not happy. She said, "Come on, Boone."

Claude told us what he knew. So there followed some discussion of the local election and the question of whether or not students would be classified as residents and allowed to vote in the mayor's race. Dr. Mirza asked Mrs. Reid if it was true that funding for the new math and science building had been eliminated. She was not at liberty to discuss it, she said, but it didn't look good.

Claude noted my height and asked if I played basketball. I said I'd played in high school and on intramural teams in college.

"Then we'll have to sign you up for the faculty team." I should have told him I'd had two surgeries on my left knee, that I couldn't run hard anymore and hadn't been very fast to start with. I did play three games on the faculty team, but my knee couldn't take it.

"Come on down to the gym," he said. "We'll do a little shoot-around and see what's what."

Dr. Oliver said he needed to be going, but then he went to the piano and played a song. Arlene explained later that he always played something, usually as everyone prepared to leave.

I was told he'd played a jazz piece by one of his favorite musicians. I don't remember the name. He had slowed it way down, they said, and people loved his arrangement.

Camille Williams said she needed to be going as well, and when she stood, so did Artis Boone.

They left, and Claude said, to nobody in particular, "I *told* Boone he ought to ease off."

"Oh, Boone can't help himself," Arlene said. "Listen, Camille may be lonely these days, but she's not that lonely. She can do a lot better than Boone, and she knows it."

"Even his wife knows that," Dr. Caruthers said.

Dr. Reid took my glass and went to the bar and poured us both another scotch.

## *18.*

"Now, Mr. Moon," he said, "there's one bit of business that I didn't want to bring up in the interview. I'm sure it won't be a problem, but we do need to talk about it, in case it does come up." He handed me the scotch.

"On the form you filled out, where it asked for your race, of course you answered white, and you clearly *are* white, there's no question about that at all, but it's necessary for us to know, in case somebody should make a formal inquiry—because these days you never know—if you have any documentation that will back that up."

"Back it up?"

"If you have any other evidence that will support your claim, any other kind of proof of being white that you can show. We're under this court order, and we can't say we've hired a white man if that's not truly the case. So help us out here. *We* know you're white."

Dr. Plant said, "No doubt in *my* mind."

"I'm not really sure. My birth certificate, I guess."

"Okay," Dr. Reid said, "that's a start, that's good, a birth certificate's good. What else you got?"

Mrs. Reid said, "Wallace Lee."

He smiled at her and then he looked back at me.

Nobody spoke.

Finally, I said, "I don't really know. I'm just *white*," and apparently that was very funny.

Dr. Caruthers said, "Yes you are, baby"—she patted me on the arm—"and don't you worry about it. It's all right."

They all laughed, and I laughed too, but I did not know what was happening.

*19.*

I had to learn my place, and I had to remember it, and that was fine with me. It was easy enough to do. I was junior faculty, I was young, I knew nothing about the college or its history.

The first time I heard someone use the term HBCU, I asked what it stood for, and the way people looked at me made it clear I needed to speak less and pay closer attention.

At a faculty meeting one morning in early October, I was sitting between Dr. Caruthers and Dr. George Mboso, an English professor from Nigeria who had been her student years earlier. They were like mother and son.

She had helped him attend graduate school and even paid for some of it, I was told. I never really got to know him. After my first quarter, he took an administrative job at Fort Valley State College, another historically black institution, nearly two hours northwest of us.

The new vice-president—a former dean at North Carolina A&T and an old friend of Vernon Stanridge, our president—was in charge of the meeting, and he had been speaking for a while.

Dr. Caruthers leaned across me and said, "Tell me this, Dr. George. Why is it necessary to avoid a perfectly good short word and go off in search of another one that is much longer but only marginally appropriate?"

Dr. Mboso laughed and said, "He does have a certain talent." Neither had supported the hiring of the new vice-president.

Dr. Caruthers was acutely attentive to language usage and pronunciation. She had grown up in nearby Waycross, where she had acquired the language patterns of south Georgia, but she now spoke in a manner indistinguishable from that of someone broadcasting the news on network television.

She made clear to her students that the learning of what was being called standard English was vital for negotiating the wider world and achieving one's goals. It did not mean completely abandoning or being ashamed of the way one had grown up speaking. One could retain that and also acquire other habits of language. One could match language to situation. She herself was supremely at ease in the rich vernacular.

Dr. Mboso spoke a version of the King's English, and I spoke—as I still do and why not—like a white man brought up in the rural South, with vowels that tell people where I'm from.

"Listen, Moon," Dr. Caruthers once said to me, "the word *can't* should not rhyme with the word *paint*. And you lay something *on* the table, not *own* the table."

But she herself had worked so hard to change her way of speaking that she had overcorrected and sometimes could not use that long *o* even when it was called for. She might say, "I on the house," not "I own the house."

Dr. Caruthers seemed to enjoy herself when she was around me. My office was two doors down from the classroom where she usually taught, and she'd stop by often. She'd say something like "Moon, who dressed you this morning?" or "Moon, look at all this mess. Has no one taught you how to operate the trash can?" She'd wave me over to sit with her at faculty meetings. One day she asked me to pronounce the words *ink pen* because she needed a lift.

*20.*

Early in my first quarter, I realized I needed a place to hide out, and I found it on the third floor of the library—a research carrel I was able to reserve for my use only, a small windowless room.

Camille Williams unlocked my door after lunch one day and found me leaning back in the chair, shoes off, feet on the table. I awoke and almost fell.

"I'm sorry. I didn't mean to wake you."

"I wasn't asleep. I was just trying to get a little work done." I couldn't find my shoes.

"And what kind of work would that be?" She looked at the bare table. "Just figuring it all out in your head?"

"I guess you caught me."

"I guess I did. Let me tell you what I tell the students. The library is not a place for sleeping."

Most of the time when I went to the carrel, I didn't use it for sleep. I only wanted to get away from people. I often experienced deep anxiety and dread in the presence of others, whoever they might have been.

I told her I knew she was right, I knew the library was not a place for sleeping.

"And these carrels? They're at a premium. There's a waiting list. You were given preferential treatment."

"I understand, and I apologize." I said it wouldn't happen again, but that didn't turn out to be true. Day after day, she saw me there and looked straight at me and let me know she was aware of my presence.

*21.*

Dr. Reid said, "Look at it this way. If a bag boy at the Piggly Wiggly can wear a tie to work, you can too." This was my first week on campus.

I wanted to say, "That's why I went to graduate school—so I wouldn't have to dress like a bag boy at the Piggly Wiggly," but I started wearing a tie every day.

We were standing outside the student center, across from Douglass Hall, a women's dorm, next to the dining hall. Something fried was in the air—the smell of home—when the clavinet riff that kicks off "Superstition" ratcheted up from a dorm window, and I was overcome with sudden, intense gladness at being right where I was.

Somebody cranked up the volume. Dr. Reid saw my face and laughed. "Sounds like they fixing to get down. What do *you* think, doctor?"

"Doctor" was a common way of referring to a faculty member, doctorate in hand or not, and Dr. Reid had just hired me with my dissertation pending, the dissertation I would never finish.

"Yes sir, I guess so."

He put his hand on my shoulder and shook it, as if testing a piece of cheap furniture. "Say you *guess* so?"

He reached out to a passing student, who brushed his hand and was about to keep walking. "Miss Raiford," he said, "do you know Mr. Everett Moon here? He's new to us, in psychology."

She said it was a pleasure to meet me and hurried off.

"That young lady is one of our best. She'll do big things."

The next morning, in my first class, there she was, four seats from the front, and she was all business. I called the roll, handed out the syllabus, and told the class their assignment for the day was to obtain a copy of the text. I didn't care whether they bought it or borrowed it, but they would need a copy, and I'd be checking the next day to see who had one.

From the back of the room, a voice said, "I won't have mine." Several other voices agreed. They would not have the book by tomorrow. Financial aid was backed up, and they couldn't buy their books until they had the money.

"All right," I said, "but you will need it. You can't pass the class without owning a book." That turned out not to be true, not for my class anyway. Books were often shared.

The door opened, and a young man eased into the room in a kind of jaunty sliding action. He made his way to a folding chair set against the back wall. I checked the roster and asked him his name.

"I'm Lawrence Walker," he said. "People call me Grip."

Somebody called out, "*Grip*," and Grip threw up his hand and said, "All right, now."

A young woman asked how much the textbook cost. I examined my complimentary copy of the book and couldn't find a price and said I didn't know.

"It's thirty-five dollars," Miss Raiford said, "and they don't have any used ones," and the way she looked at me made it clear she wanted to know why she was doing *my* job.

## 22.

I was puzzled by comments on my student evaluations: "a joke" and "can't teach" and "doesn't belong here." These comments were recorded and shown to me in October, part of a mid-quarter evaluation recently instituted by the college.

I told one of my classes I wanted us to have a talk about how I was doing as a teacher. I told them I had read their comments and wanted to ask them what I could do to improve. A male student in the back, Andrew Stubbs, was whispering in an animated way to the young woman beside him.

"How about you, Mr. Stubbs?" I said. "What do you think?"

He sat up straight and looked like he was tasting something bitter.

"You seem to have an opinion."

"Look here," he said, "my name is not Stubbs."

I picked up the roster and walked toward the back of the room. "Do I have you confused with someone else?"

"You sho nuff does."

Students laughed and twisted around in their seats to look at him. "All right," I said. "Let's put it this way: When I assign your grade, which name should I record it next to?"

"Stubbs, but that's not my name. Andrew Stubbs is a slave name. I use it but it's not mine. It belongs to your people."

"That's a legitimate way to feel," I said. "What would you like to be called?"

"I don't need you to tell me if it's legitimate or not. I don't need your approval. My African name is Jamal Malik."

From behind me, a female voice said, “Please.”

I told the young man I had no problem calling him whatever he wanted to be called. I asked him if there was anything else he wanted to say.

“Yeah. Why you teaching this class? Do you think we *need* you?”

I had turned to walk back to the front of the classroom when the voice spoke again. It was Portia Davison, a student in her thirties. “This is our professor,” she said, “and you need to show some respect.”

“*Respect*? Who you think you talking to?”

“I'm talking to *you*, Andy Stubbs.”

That set the whole class into loud motion. I heard the word *respect* spoken in various forms of mimicry and thrown back and forth, and people playing with the name Andy. The class grew louder. I tried to quiet them. I told them to hold it down, but I finally had to shout, and it got quieter. Andrew Stubbs had gone back to whispering to the student beside him.

“All right. Why did I come here? It was the only job I could get. Do I think you need me? No, I don't. I *know* you don't need me. You just need somebody to teach this class, and it doesn't have to be me. But look, everybody knows I was hired because of the suit against the college. They had to hire a white person on short notice, and so they hired me, and when they did, I was surprised. I *was*. I don't understand it myself. I'm sure they could have found somebody more qualified. I think they must have been desperate. Does that answer your questions?”

“Yassuh, it sho do. We is happy now and feels like dancing.”

Portia Davison was on her feet. "What I want to know is this: if you're so black and proud, why do you break out in a *minstrel* act for this white man? He may be enjoying it, for all *you* know, but I'm not"—she picked up her books—"and I'm not going to listen to it." She headed for the door.

I said, "Ms. Davison," but she went on out, and as she did, Jamal Malik half-shouted, "Handkerchief-head Aunt Jemima." He stood up, a few others stood, and the whole class started to leave. The period was almost over, and I didn't try to stop them.

Dr. Reid summoned me to his office right after class and told me to shut the door. "You let that boy tell you what you can call him? His mama and daddy *gave* him that name. That's who he *is*. He can be somebody else when he grows up, but right now, when they paid the money to send him here? He's Andrew Stubbs. I know his people, and I plan to give them a call. But look here"—he jabbed his finger at me—"you better get yourself some *spine*, boy."

*23.*

Two hours later, Dr. Reid stepped into my office and asked if we wanted to walk over to Miss Mary's for lunch. Walter Bonner was sitting across from my desk. I asked what was on the menu—a lame joke—and Dr. Reid ignored me.

Miss Mary's served nearly the same thing every day—a rich buffet of baked ham, baked chicken, fried chicken, and fried fish, with macaroni and cheese, creamed corn, green beans, mashed potatoes, fried okra, black-eyed peas, collard greens, dinner rolls and cornbread and banana pudding and pecan pie, and always the very sweet iced tea Miss Mary was famous for. The iced tea was special. Some days there was fried fatback, a treat of pure nostalgia for me. My grandmother used to cook it for my grandfather, and from the time I was small, he would share it with me.

Dr. Reid said, "I have a class at one o'clock. If we're going, we need to go."

"All right by me," I said. "How about you, Walt? You up for some fatback?"

"Look, *I'm* going," Dr. Reid said. "If y'all are coming along, let's go. I can't be late for my class, like some people," a reference to my bad habit of walking into class a few minutes after it should have begun.

*24.*

Walter Bonner was my best white friend in those early days at the college. He was my age, we were both new to the job, and our offices were on the same floor in Ayers Hall.

He was born in Kentucky, but grew up in Minnesota with his mother and her parents. He was eight years old when he moved there, after his father died in an odd accident.

Walt had a PhD in English from Cornell. He and his wife, Lisa, lived in faculty housing. She worked in the registrar's office. I had taken the only job I could get, but Walt had not. He was gone after a year.

We walked beside the dirt road that cut through the middle of campus. It would be paved maybe eight years later and eventually closed to allow construction of a plaza with trees and a fountain and comfortable, shaded benches. That day, it was a strip of mud and deep tire ruts where puddles from last night's rain caught the sun at noon and shone like coppery glass.

Walt was short and wide—5'5" at the most, about two-twenty. He was pale, his skin splotched pink and red, especially about the nose, which made him seem like a heavy drinker, though he wasn't. His stringy brown hair fell below his shoulders, and he usually tied it in a ponytail. Most days he wore a headband and dressed in a T-shirt and jeans.

When I told him what Dr. Reid had said to me about the way I dressed, Walt said that wearing a tie, for our generation, was an inauthentic thing to do and another subordination of substance to style—his main criticism of the college.

I wondered why Dr. Reid had not said to Walt what he had said to me.

There were quite a few people ahead of us in the serving line, but it moved quickly. We sat ourselves at the end of one of the long tables. Dr. Reid bowed his head and said a brief silent grace. A week earlier, I had heard him give a talk about the role of missionaries to the South during Reconstruction which made clear that he was not a man of faith. His wife attended Christ Chapel AME without him, but he always said grace.

The door whined open, and two men joined the serving line. They taught at the college, but I didn't know them. They saw Dr. Reid and pointed a greeting.

Both men had the substantial Afro of the day. The taller man wore a beige suit and a black shirt with an open collar neatly spread and pressed flat against his jacket lapels, and a gold shark's tooth hung from his neck. The other wore a light green short-sleeve dress shirt and a brown clip-on tie.

The men made their way to a table on the far side of the room. I asked Dr. Reid who they were.

"That's Carney and Garrison," he said. "Business Department. Joined at the hip like you and the doctor here."

He applied clear pepper sauce to his greens and handed the bottle to me.

"I never did get to ask you about that memo," Walt said. "Now I can ask Dr. Reid."

"Ask me what now?"

Walt pulled the paper from his back pocket and tried to flatten it against the table and got it wet. "This memo from the president. This mandatory meeting tomorrow, for all faculty and staff. It says there's an emergency meeting, scheduled for eleven o'clock, and it says all offices are to be closed and all classes canceled."

"Oh, that."

"But what's the emergency?"

Miss Mary Ellison, who must have been eighty-five years old, was moving slowly toward our table, a plastic pitcher in her hand.

"*Just* the lady I want to see," Dr. Reid said, "*my* sweetheart. When you gon' do me right, Miss Mary? I been waiting all these years, you pretty thing." He reached out a hand to her, and she slapped it away.

"Wallace Lee Reid, I ain't studying you." She poured iced tea in his glass, then laid her hand on his shoulder, and he covered it with his own.

"How you been, Miss Mary?"

She looked like she was welling up with tears, and maybe she was, but she always looked like that because of some problem with her eyes. "I'm fine," she said, "I'm fine."

She turned to Walt and me. "And how are you young gentlemen today?"

We both said we were doing well, and we hoped she was too. Walt said, "It's such a nice day."

She smiled at Dr. Reid. "That's what they tell me."

*25.*

That first year, I was so uncomfortable and unsure of myself in the classroom, I found ways to avoid teaching. The big three time-wasting topics certain to provoke lively class discussions were sex, religion, and race, all of which I could justify as related to psychology.

It was easy to elicit opinions about sex, and people always had things to say about religion—a subject that brought forth a surprising degree of certainty—but race was the most reliable topic for engaging a class, especially if I made myself available as a representative white man. And what choice did I have? I was *there* as a white man. That's *exactly* why I was there.

"If you had to describe white people with one word," I once asked—for no good reason; it just popped into my head—"what word would you choose?"

Sheila Tillman, sitting near the front of the class, answered without hesitation.

"*Rude*."

"*Rude*," delivered so quickly and with such force, as if requiring no thought, was not what I had expected to hear. Other answers followed, and the discussion lasted for the rest of the class. I wanted to hear what else Sheila Tillman had to say but I never did.

*26.*

Walt and I became friends with Jarvis Dollar, a twenty-seven-year-old student who had fought in Vietnam with the infantry. He invited Walt and me over to the house he rented next to campus.

We'd drink that sweet TJ Swann wine—one variation was Mellow Days and another was Easy Nights—and we might also get high.

Jarvis lived alone, but people were always at his house. A student named Danielle stayed there much of the time. She was nobody's girlfriend, but she ruled the house. She could have anything she wanted.

Jarvis was one of the students selected by an anonymous benefactor for generous financial assistance. The criteria for selection were known only to the benefactor. Jarvis had no idea why he'd been chosen. He thought it might have had something to do with his being a veteran. Many people believed the benefactor to be a wealthy white man who owned the local farm equipment factory.

I remember sinking down in the broken springs of the old sofa, listening to "Hearts Afire" and starting to feel like I'd reached a place from which I never wanted to move. I opened my eyes to find Jarvis and Danielle laughing at me.

She said, "Doc is out of it."

Jarvis said, "We need to get you some coffee before you go to class."

"Class? He got another class?" She shook her head. "I don't *know*."

## *27.*

Dr. Reid called me into his office and told me to shut the door. I took a seat across from his desk, and he leaned forward, elbows resting on his immaculate workspace.

"I'm going to tell you something, and you won't like it, but I don't care if you like it or not. You need to hear it."

There was a knock on the door. Mrs. Wells, the division secretary, walked in and handed a paper to Dr. Reid and one to me. "I'll need this by noon tomorrow," she said. "Keep a copy for yourself. Why y'all locked up in here?"

Dr. Reid gave a leisurely point in my direction.

Mrs. Wells fixed me with weary eyes. "And *where* is your monthly report?" she asked me. "And why can't you get it in on time like everybody else?"

"I'm not the only one," I said.

"You're the only one *you* need to worry about."

I told her I was sorry and I'd get it to her before the day was over. She turned back to Dr. Reid. "And that other thing? That's been put off till next week. Apparently, the requisition has been held up. I'm calling around to see what we can do."

"That's not really much of a surprise, is it?" he said. "But thank you, Mrs. Wells. I appreciate your staying on it. Just let me know."

When she'd gone, I asked Dr. Reid what it was that had been put off.

He said, "Did nobody ever teach you that it's impolite to ask about things that don't concern you? Did you have no home training at all?"

"I thought it *might* concern me."

"Look here," he said. "You've got things that *do* concern you that you do need to be thinking about. Like whether you want to continue teaching here or not. How about that?

"Let me ask you this: why am I working so much harder than you are? I *thoroughly* prepare for my classes, I *always* meet them on time, I *stay* on schedule, and I demand that the students do the work, and I don't cut them any slack. They're *here* to get an education. You follow me now?"

"Yes, sir."

"And *never*, not *one* time, not in *all* the years I have been a teacher, have I set foot in my class when I was intoxicated. Do you hear me talking to you?"

"Yes, sir."

"Mr. Moon, do you hear me talking to you now?

"Yes, sir. I do."

"I *expect* to see a change, or you won't be with us much longer, and you need to understand that. I tell you what—you need to talk to your friend Bonner. He knows how to conduct himself like a professional. You go talk to him and tell him what I told you, see if he doesn't agree with me."

I said I would, but I didn't.

*28.*

Faculty members were evaluated on teaching, research, service, and professional development. Though I was never a good teacher, over the years I did learn how to get better teaching evaluations from students.

I made my expectations clear, I covered a modest amount of material in an orderly way, I allowed class discussions to range far off topic, and I inflated my grades.

For my research credentials, I was supposed to be working on a paper about William James. After a while, I claimed to be working on a book. Nobody believed that. I did have lots of notes and a few written pages.

Dr. Reid knew quite a bit about William James. When I told him what I was working on, he said he thought it was a good idea.

Claude Jackson was the one who encouraged me to write the paper on William James. *The Varieties of Religious Experience* was supplementary reading for his philosophy class.

My service credentials were documented by any scrap of paper that attested to the slightest thing I had done for students, other faculty, the college, or the community—a shamefully bloated dossier of mediocrity, claiming credit for things I was required to do anyway.

These were presented as achievements, as was mere attendance at other events. I once saved a funeral program, thinking I might use it to document my community involvement, but I summoned the decency not to do that.

I worked hardest at mastering the illusion of substance in organizational language. Another way to say this is that I developed a facility for the goal-related generation, implementation, assessment, and results-based modification of verbal structures designed to facilitate the acquisition of positive academic sanctions likely to impact remuneration and retention. Language like that.

But when it came to professional development, I was in trouble, since I hadn't completed the PhD. I tried to compensate by attending every professional meeting I could afford to attend, having often devised some way to get my name on the program, even if I did not actually participate, as sometimes I did not.

The program with my name on it was the document I needed for my dossier. I was good at writing abstracts and getting on panels where most of the work could be done by other participants. Sometimes I fell ill at meetings. Sometimes in the hotel bar.

All this devious effort fooled no one. I clearly did not meet the standards set forth by the Board of Regents for either promotion or tenure. I'd never finished my doctorate, I'd published nothing, and I could show only modest service to the college or community. Even so, I'd managed to put together a long letter of application detailing my many accomplishments, supported by a file swollen with paper claiming to be documentation.

Dr. Reid intervened to alter the effects of negative assessments by committees at each level. I kept my job only because he saw to it that I did. He removed me from the tenure track and arranged a series of one-year contracts, although technically this arrangement was a violation of board policy. He obtained a special waiver for me, or so I was told. In the end he came to believe this was not his finest achievement. It was a source of regret.

## *29.*

The only place large enough to hold the president's meeting was the gym, but the roof was being repaired again, so we crammed into the auditorium of the science building, a steep amphitheater smelling faintly of sulfur and formaldehyde. The weather had turned cold, the heat was on, the room too hot. We were wedged into the rows of desks; chairs had been added in the aisles, and people stood along the walls. The heat intensified the lab smells, which mingled with perfume and cologne and stale smoke in clothes, and there was some kind of pungent spice worn only by the Africans.

Walt and I sat in the middle row, halfway to the top of the amphitheater. I wondered if we smelled like wet chickens. Tiffany Raiford had told me that Mandinka elders taught their young people to detect the white man's presence by his odor, which was said to resemble a wet chicken's.

We saw Dr. Reid sitting in the first row beside his wife, who would be taking the minutes. Dr. Caruthers and Dr. Mboso came in and sat directly behind us. Camille Williams slipped past to join a man I didn't know. She smelled like the cool air after a good rain.

Dr. Vernon Stanridge was in his fifties, a former athlete who still displayed an economy and ease in how he moved. He stepped to the podium, and people quieted down. He said, "Good morning," and the room resounded with "Good morning."

Dr. Stanridge occasionally began a meeting with a prayer, but not this time. "Ladies and gentlemen," he said, "I thank all of you for taking time out of your busy schedules to come here today. I would not have asked you to do so had there not been an urgent need. Can everybody hear me? Can you hear me up there in the back, Mr. Hitchcock?"

A flat voice answered with "Yes sir," the words delivered slowly and without enthusiasm, and this drew a laugh from the assembly. Dr. Stanridge laughed too, and he pointed in the direction of the voice. I looked back but couldn't tell who had spoken. There were maintenance workers standing all along the back wall.

"I have called the college family together this morning because of a serious matter that needs the attention of each and every one of us. We operate here *as* a family, and what affects one of us affects us all.

"Now, I remember one day when I was a boy, I came home with a bad mark on my report card, a bad grade in my conduct at school, or what we called deportment back then. I can't remember exactly what it was I had done, but when I got home with a bad mark in deportment, my daddy gave me *another* bad mark or two. Yes, he did, and when he was finished, he said something to me I never forgot. He told me I had to understand that when I got a bad conduct grade, the whole *family* got a bad conduct grade.

"So today, well, that's what has happened. We have received a bad grade—I have and you have, all of us have—with respect to some aspects of our finances. I have already been taken to the woodshed on this by the Board of Regents, but I'm afraid there's more pain on the way. We're going to have to cut our budget by a significant amount—$230,000, at a minimum, which will mean cuts in personnel and operating expenses. This involves a freeze in salaries, so there will be no raise for next year."

The room groaned, and people began talking. The president said, "I know, I know," and he nodded and kept nodding, and he raised his hand no higher than his head and he held it there, as if waiting to be called on. The noise subsided, and he said, "Now, I know you have questions" and pointed toward a man in the second row. "Dr. Cates?"

Dr. Anthony Cates, a sociologist active in campus politics and vocal on every issue, stood and began to speak in a voice just below a shout. "Mr. President," he said, "you tell me I will have *no* increase in salary. You say that we are *all* at fault. I am *not* at fault, sir. I have *no* ability to make decisions about the budget. *You*"—he punched his finger at the president—"*you* make these decisions, up in the *big* house." This drew moans, and Dr. Cates looked around, seeming puzzled and irritated. "That's where these decisions are made, not down in the lowly Department of Sociology."

"Lord help us the day *that* happens," Dr. Caruthers muttered, and she jabbed the back of my shoulder.

Numerous people had raised their hands. The president nodded his assurance of recognition at several of them. "Dr. Cates," he said, "I appreciate your comments. You are of course correct that we in the administration are the ones who make decisions on fiscal matters, and we do bear primary responsibility for problems in those areas. I apologize if I seemed to say something other than that. All of us, however, participate in spending the funds allocated, and sometimes we have gone beyond our means. I think you would have to agree with that."

Dr. Cates was still standing. "I do *not* agree. Those of us…"

The president pointed toward one of the raised hands. "I'm going to recognize Dr. Fulton."

Dr. Cates said, "Mr. President…"

Dr. Stanridge patted the air. "Dr. Cates, thank you for your input. We do appreciate it. We need to hear from everybody on this matter, so we need to move on. But thank you. Dr. Fulton?"

The man who rose to speak, Dr. Gerard Fulton, was a professor of agricultural engineering. "Thank you, Mr. President. I'll be brief. The need for budget cuts seems to be a foregone conclusion, a mandate from the Board. I cannot speak for the rest of this group and would not presume to do so, but I'm fairly certain that most of us would wish to have some say in this matter. That is, we would ask that these decisions not be made by the administration and simply handed down to us. I suggest an advisory committee be formed to make recommendations to you and your staff and that there be further discussions before final decisions are made that may negatively impact the academic soundness of this institution." As he spoke the last words, he was taking his seat.

The president gave no indication of how he felt about the proposal. "We will take that under advisement, Dr. Fulton."

He pointed toward Dr. Vikram Patel, who merely said he wanted to associate himself with Dr. Fulton's comments. Dr. Patel was a biologist, one of several Indian professors, a man respected for his intellect and his quietly forceful manner. Dr. Patel became my friend and someone I admired. He was also someone who, years later, would play a small part in the events surrounding my dismissal from the college.

The president said, "I'm going to recognize Mrs. Bailey, way in the back there. Mrs. Bailey, I notice you've had your hand up all this time. How are you today?"

"I'm fine, Dr. Stanridge. Thank you. I just want to piggyback on Dr. Cates's comment. Now, everybody in this room *knows* me, and everybody knows I speak my mind even if folks don't like what I have to say. Now, it may be true, and I'm sure it is, that we all bear some responsibility; sometimes we go over budget. I know we do in the bookstore, but when we do, *y'all* let us know about it. The business office sends me a note or a printout or somebody calls me *up*, and then I'm supposed to find some money somewhere else in my budget and shift it over there to handle the problem. Am I right?"

She looked around the room.

"But the college is running a deficit of almost a quarter of a million dollars, and y'all just found out about it? See now, I don't *understand* that. If somebody from the business office knows when the bookstore is $200 in the red, how could the whole college go so far over budget and nobody do anything to stop it, and now we're the ones who have to make it up? So that's what I want to know: how did this happen?"

When she sat down, a few people clapped.

"You've raised a fair question, Mrs. Bailey," the president said, "and I thank you for doing so." There was a trickle of laughter. "But it's not an easy question to answer, and the answer I am obliged to give you now is embarrassing, it really is, because I have to plead ignorance. I don't exactly know what happened. It seems like we just zigged when we shoulda zagged."

Dr. Caruthers drove her knuckle into my shoulder. "That's just pitiful."

"We made some wrong moves," the president said. "We certainly did. But let's be clear about this: no money went into anybody's pocket. We're not talking about any foul play. We messed up. We counted wrong, we guessed wrong, we made some bad projections."

Dr. Reid raised his hand and was recognized. He asked his question without standing. "Will the audit be made public?"

"Well now, Wallace Lee"—and here the president slipped into some other mode of speaking—"that ain't for me to say. That's up to the Board. We all got somebody to answer to. You got your big house, and I got mine. Am I right, Dr. Cates?"

Dr. Reid stood and turned sideways, and he addressed the whole room in a slow and deliberate manner. "I want the minutes to *show*"—he looked down at Mrs. Reid—"that I am making a request of the president to ask the Board of Regents for the full audit to be made *public*, since we need to understand the ways in which we have gone wrong, and we need to take action to correct them. Will you make that request to the Board on our behalf, Dr. Stanridge?"

The president executed a quick return from his playful way of speaking—what Dr. Reid would later call his "country mode." "We will certainly take your request under advisement. Now we need to move on with the matter at hand."

He proceeded to give details about the cuts to be made. People raised their hands, but the president called on no one else, and when he had finished, the meeting was over.

## *30.*

Dr. Reid and I stood on the back steps of Ayers Hall, sharing his unfiltered Camels. It was late afternoon, the smell of burning leaves in the air. We could hear the snare drums of band practice on the far side of campus.

"See, you're still young"—he took off his glasses, held them up for inspection, and put them back on—"and so time, to you, is almost the way it is to the children,"—by children, he meant the college students we taught—"the way it is to everybody when they're young."

We'd been talking about the war in Vietnam, and then about World War II.

"It's a fact," he said. "Call it a psychological fact, if you have to, if there *is* such a thing." He did not hold psychology in high esteem. "When you get older, the past comes closer. That's just the way it is. For these young people—I'm not saying you, now, but for them—World War II might as well be the Civil War."

He stepped on his cigarette, picked it up, and began to field-strip it. "I was in the Philippines. And you say your daddy was in the Philippines?"

"Yes sir, that's right."

He crushed the stub between his fingers, crumbled the last bits of tobacco and let them fall, rolled up the tiny scrap of paper and slipped it into his coat pocket.

"You know what?" he said. He squinted and then he seemed to be peering far down the road. "I just remembered something, right this minute. When I was on the troop ship coming home, I met this white soldier who'd lost an arm. The boy was from Quitman, not too far from where I grew up. Down around...but you know where it is, right?" I did.

"I knew him for a few days. We talked some. We knew some of the same places. We laughed a few times. Then one morning I went to see him, and they said he'd died during the night. You know, I had forgotten all *about* that boy."

The drums came to an abrupt stop. I told him the only thing I knew about my father's service in the Philippines, a story my mother had told us. When the war ended, he was on Luzon, on CQ duty. They made the surrender announcement to the troops at a USO show, and he heard the shout far off, and then he heard the celebration coming toward him. He knew what it had to be.

"I remember that day," Dr. Reid said. "I remember right where I was. I was playing five-card stud in the motor pool. I had a pair of kings. They said the war was over, just like that, but you couldn't get it through your head. It was hard thing to believe. When it happened, though, I was holding a pair of kings."

Far across the yard, the band started up again, and the bugles joined the drums, but they warbled off key—a weak sound, and sad.

## *31.*

The Monroe public library holds an annual old book sale, and that's where I find a single volume (Richard to Tides) of *The World Book*'s first edition, printed in 1917.

Also the 1919 yearbook of Pine Hill High School, in which the odd photos appear to be cutouts pasted onto the page, full-body images maybe an inch tall, with faces that can't be distinguished from one another. Most seem to be posed, some comically, as if dancing or running, some seriously, as if lecturing or standing at attention.

I've paid for the books, and I'm heading for the door when there's a tap on my arm.

"Are you blind, or what?"

It's Tammy Callaway, from high school.

"Don't be sneaking up on an old man, Tammy."

"I didn't know you were a *book* fan. Let me see what you've got there." She grabs the yearbook. "What in the world?" She shoves it back into my hands.

I ask about her family.

"Well, I guess you already know about Jimmy"—but I don't, I don't even know who Jimmy is—"and after Daddy died, we moved Mama in with us for a few years, and now she's gone too. At least we never had to put her in Lake Valley. Working out there as long as I have, and seeing what kind of life it is? I couldn't have stood that.

"Oh, but you know who was out there until just recently? Claire Hartley. She fell and broke her hip not too long after Leon died—but I'm sure you know that—and she never did really recover. She was in Lake Valley for about two years.

"She had pictures of Junior all over her room, all around the bed and on the dresser and the shelves. I used to go in and talk to her all the time. She got to where she couldn't say anything, but she'd listen to me. She enjoyed me being there."

"I'm sure she did, Tammy."

"She was bad-off towards the end, though, one of the worst I've seen. She didn't even know where she was. She didn't seem to know anything."

I move toward the door, and Tammy moves with me. She asks if I ever hear from Suzanne.

"No, I never do."

I say it was good to see her, and then I'm out the door. She yells something, but I can't make out what it is.

*32.*

Suzanne was fascinated by weather. She didn't understand why that wasn't true of everybody. I used to tease her, saying she would probably marry a weatherman. She owned books on cloud formations. She liked to read about extreme weather, like tornadoes and hurricanes and droughts and floods, and about optical phenomena—sunsets and rainbows and witch water and mirages. And when we drove out through the countryside at dusk, she was always in search of the green flash.

Suzanne had transferred to our school in my junior year. She was sharp and funny. Nothing defeated her. She got good grades but didn't seem to care much about that. She was a champion speller, she was athletic, she could play the piano. And there was also a wary intelligence about her, a cautious, observing quality that let you know she was nobody's fool. The day she appeared in the classroom, I couldn't stop looking at her. She never looked at me at all.

*33.*

In my senior year I had hoped to play well enough to get a basketball scholarship to a small college or a junior college. I spent a lot of time in the gym that summer. But in the eighth game of the season, I made a cut to the basket and ripped the ligaments out of my left knee, and I was out for the year.

The scholarship was unlikely to happen, even if I'd been healthy. But the summer before my senior year, I worked hard to improve my game and give myself an outside chance. My job sweeping up at the cotton mill was on the first shift, six to two. I'd go home and eat and rest for a while, and then

I'd head for the gym, which was normally locked in the summer, but Coach Morris had given me a key.

He had also given one to Suzanne's brother, Leon, Jr., who was sure to be a starter in his sophomore year. The varsity had scrimmaged his freshman team, and he'd been the best player on the court.

When I showed up, he would already be there. I didn't want to have to talk to anybody, but he had no interest in talking either. We worked out on opposite ends of the court.

My routine involved laps and sprints, but mostly shooting the ball. I'd go around the horn, shooting jump shots. I'd run the court, then shoot free throws. At the end of the day, I tried not to quit until I had made ten in a row, so I had some long afternoons. It didn't always happen.

Leon's routine centered less on shooting and more on drills that would improve his defensive play and rebounding and conditioning. He'd run the court backwards, using crossover steps, and do this at impressive speed. He did want me to work with him on his outlet passes for the fast break. He'd grab a rebound and hit me at different distances as I broke downcourt.

We'd go through our workout routines, and then at the end of the afternoon, we'd play one-on-one, make it-take it, first-to-ten-baskets-wins, win-by-two. One day in late July, we were in a tough game—the score was 9-8, his way—when Suzanne walked in.

This was before she and I started going out. I looked at her and froze, and Leon drove past me and won the game.

"Time to go, Junior."

She held out her hands for the ball.

He threw her a bounce pass, and she put up a ridiculous shot from about twenty feet, slung it from her right hip, a line-drive throw that slammed hard against the backboard and went in, and we all cracked up.

Suzanne's laughter ran through me like a shock and made me want to hear it again.

I retrieved the ball and threw it back to her. She shot it again with the same motion, and it missed everything and that was hilarious too.

*34.*

Suzanne had broken up with Bill McMillan at the beginning of the summer. They'd dated almost a year. Bill had told people they'd probably end up getting married. When she told him she didn't want to be with him anymore, Bill couldn't handle it. He accused her of already having another boyfriend, though she didn't, not then, and he swore that he'd find out who it was. He followed her, watched her from a distance, called her house to find out if she was home.

"You should see some of the letters he writes," she told me. "They're like threatening love notes."

"He threatens you?"

"Maybe that's not the right word. He doesn't threaten me physically. He says nothing matters anymore, he doesn't care if the whole world explodes—things like that. He says he can't stand to look at the places we went together, and he wants to burn them down."

When Suzanne and I first started going out, we liked it being a secret. What we felt was special. We had no desire to share it with anyone else. We'd drive to Covington or Lawrenceville to go to a movie or get a hamburger—not to Athens, where we'd see people we knew. We liked taking long drives, whether we were going anywhere or not. We didn't mind getting lost.

The day she told me about Bill's letters, we'd driven south out of town in my grandfather's used Corvair. We took a left onto a road neither of us was familiar with.

The road went downhill, with sharp turns and switchbacks like a mountain road, then straightened out onto flat land that went on and on. When dusk became night, it felt like we were on a bridge that cut across a dark lake stretching out for miles on either side.

"So you're still getting letters?"

"Yeah. I just wish he would stop, you know? He's a good guy, or he used to be. He can find somebody else and be happy. I told him that, but..."

"Maybe I need to say something to him."

"No," she said, "don't do that." She lifted her head from my shoulder and sat up straight. "And anyhow, Junior already told him to leave me alone."

"And he's still doing it?"

"I guess I don't really know. It's only been a few days since Junior talked to him. Maybe he'll quit."

"What did Leon say to him?"

"I don't know exactly. I asked him, but he wouldn't tell me. He made me promise to tell him if I got another letter, but I'm not sure if I will. Tell him, I mean."

The next afternoon, I couldn't make a basket. Nothing would go in. I had no touch. I could have been wearing winter gloves. I walked down to Leon's end of the court and asked him what he'd said to Bill McMillan.

"I told him he was a better man than the way he'd been acting. I told him the only hope he had was to give up, just to let it go. That was the only way she'd ever come back to him, I said, but even then, I said, she probably won't."

"What did he say?"

"He asked me where she was, right then, and I told him he had to stop asking that question. If you don't, I said, she's going to end up hating you, and you don't want that. And if you do keep on making her afraid, I said, I'm going to kick the shit out of you."

"You told him that?"

"Yeah. He wanted to go ahead and fight, but I told him I didn't want to fight him.  I said we had all liked him, the whole family—which is true, we liked him a lot—but I said he had to leave her alone now. That's what a strong man would do, I told him. A *strong* man would have the guts to suck it up and let her go. He might have heard me then. I'm not sure, but I think maybe he did."

Leon was one of those rare players who can lift a team just by the intensity of the way they move. He was a tenacious defender. He had uncanny anticipation of rebounds and passes. That year, he carried us to the state tournament in Macon, where they held the games on a makeshift court in the City Auditorium. If you shot from the corner, you risked hitting the balcony that hung out over the court. Sudden dead spots on the floor caused turnovers.

We won the first game—Leon had eleven assists and four steals and nine rebounds—then lost in the second round to Toccoa Falls, a team with two all-state players. But Leon was still the best one on the court.

*35.*

Dr. Reid left his papers to Howard University. I'm cramming most of mine into trash bags, and here's what occurs to me. I could donate the few items I'm saving to some local concern, maybe even some place that's no longer in existence. I could leave them jointly to Bell's Cafe and to Perry Garrett's Barbecue. I could dedicate them to the black and white people of Monroe who still remember those places. I hereby do so. You know who you are.

The day feels clean, one of those fall mornings when the sharp air quickens the heart like a little surprise. The sky looks washed and brushed dry, blue in layers. I'm sitting at a sidewalk table, looking toward the Troy Theater, torn down years ago after it burned, looking through the ghost of the old facade, and it gives a shape to the morning blue that isn't there.

*36.*

Live Action TV news from Atlanta. A man is half a step outside his apartment, and he looks away, a hand over his face.

The young white woman leans down. "Mr. Mercado." The camera eases lower. "Sir, we're here to speak with you about..."—she touches his wrist—"about the Jesus...you know, about the vision?"

The wind throws a breathy rattle through the microphone. There's a bad scar under his right eye, all the way to his ear. His skin is bruised tan, the temple above the scar is sunken. "But it was...*Nuestra Senora*," he manages to say, "and she did not..." His mouth works into a spasm, he tries to speak and starts to shake.

"Yes, sir," she says, "that's all right, that's..." She puts a hand on his shoulder and feints toward leaving. "Sir, I apologize. We...it appears we misunderstood, and I'm so sorry, I..."

She tries to guide him back inside, but the spasm takes over, his head bobs a difficult yes as he steps through the door and pats her on the elbow. She turns her stricken look toward the camera and fights for control.

"And we *are* live...off the Buford Highway."

*37.*

A billboard on Georgia 11 reads "Mental Illness Touches Every Family." In the strip mall below it, a giant balloon man with a cigarette body flails at the air, like a cruel visual aid.

There's a story in *The New York Times* this morning about an eleven-year-old Missouri boy who stole a dog, tied it up, duct-taped its muzzle shut, hung it from a limb and beat it with a golf club, crushed its paws with pliers, put out its eyes with a stick, dripped acid on it and kept the dog like that for three days until it finally disappointed him and died. They caught him when he went out looking for another dog.

Today, our mother would be diagnosed as bipolar, with psychotic episodes. Back then, the terminology was manic-depressive. It was the manic end of the continuum that gave her the most trouble. When she was depressed, she was paralyzed. She hid herself away and slept a lot. As far as I know, she never tried to harm herself. There were rare periods of normal behavior and emotion, when our real mother emerged. She was smart and gentle and funny, the only person who could make my grandfather laugh. She enjoyed music and she liked to sing. But the singing could be an indication of her becoming unwell. She might begin to sing all the time, and then too loudly and in places where it was not appropriate. She would start buying things she couldn't afford.

My grandparents noticed what she brought home and they kept track of receipts, so they could return things. She once came home with maybe ten dresses and twice as many pairs of shoes, and that same afternoon, a delivery truck pulled up with a grand piano.

*38.*

I was ten years old when one of the mill owners gave my grandfather some ancient golf clubs for Donnie and me. We'd go out into a field and hit shots. The clubs were real antiques, with wooden shafts and names imprinted on the irons—mashie, niblick, and spoon. The few balls in the canvas bag were misshapen and dead. We looked along the road beside the golf course and found some better ones.

When Donnie was sixteen, he got a small set of modern clubs for Christmas. He shared those with me, though neither of us played on a real course until we were grown. Back then there was no public course in town, just the country club. In my sophomore year of college, I bought some clubs at a garage sale and started playing on the university course, which was free to students.

I still own a set of clubs, which are now stored in Donnie's garage. He's not really a golfer, but he plays a round at the public course occasionally. He's helping me load a few boxes into my car when he steps back into the garage and points at the golf bag.

He says, "I see you got a 1-iron in there. What's *that* about?" He pulls out the club and steps over into the yard and takes a few swings.

"It's yours if you want it, and the other clubs too. I won't be using them. I don't even know why I held on to them."

"I'm going out this Friday," he says, "me and Hubert. Why don't you come along? He's a member at that new place."

He knows I'm not up to it, though. And even if I was, I wouldn't be able to take a good swing. I can't shift my weight onto my left leg.

"Look, tell you what: why don't you just come on out and get yourself a cart and ride around with us and make know-it-all comments, then? I know you can still do that, professor. You used to do it for a living. Listen, have you seen Hubert since you got back?"

Hubert West. It's no surprise that he's a member at the new club. I've heard it takes $20,000 up front to join, but I'm sure that's no problem for Hubert, whose family has always had money, and from what I hear, he has made some good investments. I've always liked Hubert, who has been Donnie's friend since they were in high school, though afterwards they never did move in the same circles.

Donnie swings the 1-iron, chunks it into the dirt and laughs in that rasping way of his that has always made me laugh too and still does, and I wish I felt well enough to go with them.

We used to love racing barefoot across the cool grass in the back yard after supper. I remember the night we raced down the little hill, across the dirt driveway, through the gate in the chicken wire fence that served as our finish line, and I was faster than Donnie for the first time. I must have been thirteen years old. I thought no one would ever outrun me again.

*39.*

Donnie's son-in-law is addicted to methamphetamine. He's been in and out of treatment, in and out of jail. He's out of jail now, but Elizabeth doesn't want Iris near him. That's why she's staying with Donnie and Charlotte.

"Shrunk up like a goddamned mummy," Donnie says after supper tonight when it's just the two of us. The little girl has been put to bed, and Charlotte's in the kitchen.

"Got this sick-looking skin, green-like, with sores all over him. He picks at himself, digs holes in his own skin, and his teeth are gone, little brown stubs. That shit has just eaten them away. It's gon' kill him."

"Yes, it is," I said.

## *40.*

An early part of the dissertation I never finished—never really started—was a study of the effects of amphetamine on some behaviors. I wrote a proposal to investigate the results of amphetamine injections on the learning abilities of laboratory rats. I never carried out the study, but I did run a few trials to see how it might go, using a range of doses.

At high dosage, there was a chance of what the literature called "stereotyped motor behavior"—a syndrome of repetitive movements that sometimes included self-mutilation, tied to excess dopamine in the caudate nucleus.

On the last pilot trial I ran, I injected a rat with the highest dosage—the first time I had administered that dose—and put him back in his cage. I left him there for the drug to take effect while I went into another room and made sure the apparatus was set up properly. I was gone no more than two minutes.

I came back to find the rat had eaten off its paws and was gnawing a hole in its gut, shrieking as it bit into itself. I filled a syringe with Nembutal and injected all of it into the rat's heart. I sat down on the floor with the dead rat in my hand. I sat there for a while. I could not stop hearing that sound. I can hear it today.

Hadn't I known what the rat might do? I had known it, yes, but I had never imagined it. I had never let myself see it and hear it. I abandoned the project and I never undertook any other research.

*41.*

William James: "Nitrous oxide and ether, especially nitrous oxide, when sufficiently diluted with air, stimulate the mystical consciousness to an extraordinary degree. Depth beyond depth of truth seems revealed to the inhaler. This truth fades out, however...and if any words remain...they prove to be the veriest nonsense. Nevertheless, the sense of profound meaning having been there persists...."Some years ago, I myself made some observations on this aspect of nitrous oxide intoxication.... One conclusion was forced upon my mind...that our normal waking consciousness is but one special type of consciousness, whilst all about it, parted from it by the flimsiest of screens, there lie potential forms of consciousness entirely different....

"How to regard them is the question—for they are discontinuous with ordinary consciousness."

*42.*

Here's an obituary from the *New York Times* dated April 28, 1998, announcing the death of Carlos Castaneda. The writer of the obituary describes Castaneda's enormously successful and lucrative career but concludes that his life and work "played out in a wispy blur of sly illusion and artful deceit."

Not only were there the long-standing questions about the truth of his writings, always offered as non-fiction accounts of his dealings with the Yaqui sorcerer Don Juan Matus, but there were questions about his marital history, place and date of birth, and the circumstances of his death.

I lost interest in Castaneda back in the seventies, but there was a time when I trusted his writing about his transcendent experiences with Don Juan, mainly because his first book included an appendix that was a "structural scheme, abstracted from the data on the states of nonordinary reality presented in the foregoing part of this work."

This appendix, along with the narrative, served as his dissertation, for which he was awarded his doctorate in anthropology from UCLA. If UCLA's anthropologists trusted him, why shouldn't I?

But when Castaneda was supposedly in the desert, taking peyote and learning from the sorcerer, he was apparently in the library at UCLA, reading accounts of the peyote experience written by others. In the obituary, his former wife is quoted as saying that she doubts Don Juan Matus ever existed. She suspects Castaneda took the name from the cheap Portuguese wine they liked to drink, Mateus.

*43.*

After supper, Donnie and I are sitting in the TV room, and Charlotte is giving Iris a bath.

"I just remembered," he says. "The other day when I was down in the basement, I came across something I thought you might like to see. I'll go get it."

"I'll go with you."

"You might ought to stay here. Those steps are tricky."

"Let me take a look. I don't believe I've ever even been in your basement."

We walk through the kitchen and down the hall. He opens a door and flips on the light and starts down. "Whoever built this staircase didn't know what the hell they were doing, that's for sure. I've been meaning to replace it."

I can tell it's too steep for me. I walk back into the kitchen and sit at the table. When Donnie comes up, he's carrying a gray metal box I recognize, though I haven't seen it in almost fifty years. It was a Christmas present we both received one year, a shared gift that we immediately destroyed.

"Let me just set it down here," he says as he's putting the case on the table. "But maybe not, it's so dirty. I don't imagine Charlotte would appreciate it. Let's step outside."

We take a seat at the patio table, and he pries open the clasp on the box. Shards of glass fall out, along with a few test tubes, and he lays the box down flat.

There's an empty vial labeled xylene and one labeled alcohol, and there are four empty bottles with illegible labels. The two beakers are encrusted with brown grime.

"We really did ourselves proud, didn't we?" he says. "Little knuckleheads."

We had been in such a rush to make chemistry, whatever that was, out of the chemistry set, we had demolished it before Christmas day was over. Almost the only thing intact is the instruction booklet, still sealed in plastic.

## *44.*

I drive down to Social Circle and head west on I-20. Before long, traffic backs up, till the highway is as still as a junkyard. We're locked in place maybe fifteen minutes before people start to leave their cars and walk ahead and stare into the distance, where three lanes hit the horizon and nothing moves but the air warped with heat. I open the door and manage to stand. Two men are talking nearby. I hear the word *accident*. I hear the words *God help us, who knows*? When I woke up today, I'd been dreaming about a funeral. A baby was playing a sad tune on the piano, but it was not a hymn. I was sitting in a pew and wearing no shirt, eating a candy bar. When I left the church, two dogs broke toward me growling, their heads low to the ground. On the trashy strip of grass beside the interstate, a boy and a man throw a ball back and forth. All this could be a dream too. When the cars start to move again, I hear the word *miracle* spoken in a bitter tone, but we're on our way at last and somehow it feels like grace.

*45.*

Dr. Caruthers was writing a biography of Zora Neale Hurston, whom she always called Zora, as though she were a friend. In Hurston's essay "Characteristics of Negro Expression" she wrote, "If we are to believe the majority of writers of Negro dialect and the burnt-cork artists, Negro speech is a weird thing, full of 'ams' and 'Ises.' Fortunately, we don't have to believe them. We may go directly to the Negro and let him speak for himself. I know that I run the risk of being damned as an infidel for declaring that nowhere can be found the Negro who asks 'am it?' nor yet his brother who announces 'Ise uh gwinter.' He exists only for a certain type of writers and performers."

At age thirteen, Zora Neale Hurston tried to honor her mother's dying wishes not to have certain traditional practices observed upon her death, when the pillow would be removed from under her head, all the clocks and the mirrors covered, and the bed turned to face the east, as would the grave, allowing the departed to arise in the afterlife with her face to the sunrise. The girl tried to intervene, but the elders paid her no attention.

Dr. Caruthers was a very private person, and I was curious about her family situation. I asked Camille. She said Dr. Caruthers had once been married, but was divorced. I found out later that her six-year-old son had run out into the street chasing a ball and been killed by a car. She and her husband had divorced soon after. I wondered why Camille had told me about the marriage and divorce, but not about the accident.

Dr. Caruthers said, "One of the things I love about Zora is the fact that if she were asked a question about the Negro, she would say, 'Which one?' The same for white people. She saw the same virtues and vices in everyone. She said, 'In my eyesight, you lose nothing by not looking just like me.'"

*46.*

Late one Friday afternoon, Camille and I were both parked on the road in front of the Jacksons' house and we'd walked out there at the same time.

"I need to tell you something about how you carry yourself," she said. "You walk around with your head down. Why do you do that?"

"Well, so what if I do?" I wanted to say. It threw me off balance to hear something about myself I'd never realized. If I thought about it, though, it was obvious.

"Yeah. I don't know. I just do."

She said, "You need to hold your head up and look at people."

It was much later—it was years later—that I understood what she meant. She was not telling me to stand up for myself. She was saying, "Hold your head up, and when you meet somebody on the sidewalk or in the hallway, look them in the eye and acknowledge they exist."

## *47.*

The tornado hit the town at noon. Walt and I had just sat down beside a window at Miss Mary's when the room darkened and the sky at the end of Carver Drive took on a green deeper than the pines. The lights went out and came back on and went out.

The windows rattled, lightning struck somewhere near, a blast of silver-black rain and wind hit us, blew out the windows and shifted the walls and a giant groaning arose and then it was gone.

The rain collapsed. People climbed from under the tables. I looked down Carver Drive and saw trees across the road. I saw a truck flipped on its side. Walt and I made our way back to Ayers Hall.

The infirmary had lost its roof, and the tall oaks along the west side of the quadrangle formed a perfect column of damage, as if systematically vandalized, each tree mangled and broken, three of the six uprooted.

Half of Royal Pines Manor was a flattened expanse of trash, the bright mud and shattered glass blinking with vehicles' flashing lights. Some of the mobile homes looked like they had been crushed underfoot. Others were simply missing. My trailer appeared untouched.

People gathered at the laundromat, in the center of the property, next to where the small office had been. The park manager, a white man named Harold Burton, stood in front of the laundromat, talking with several people, one of whom was the sheriff. With sweeping arm movements, they seemed to be describing the course the storm had taken. The entire west side of Royal Pines Manor's quarter-mile oval had been leveled.

The trailer park was new, open for six months when I moved in. It had been carved out of an old pecan orchard—no pines anywhere near—and the trees just beyond the park now looked as if they had been decorated as part of some demented celebration. They were hung with strips of metal and all kinds of paper trash, ragged with insulation and cotton and foam.

I saw a tire speared on an intact limb, like the successful ring-toss of something unaware it was playing a game.

I walked over to Harold Burton, who frowned at me and turned back to the sheriff. "What good they think that'll do," the sheriff said, "I don't know. Strap a guy wire on your trailer to keep a tornado from blowing it away. That's foolish." He turned to me. "One of these yours?"

"No, I'm back on this other side. Was anybody hurt?"

Harold Burton said, "You didn't *hear*?" He looked at me with hostile disbelief. "*Killed* a little girl, two years old. One of these Rodriguez children over here." He pointed toward a slab of concrete, nothing on it now but a large tree limb.

"The ambulance was just here. One other child, but he's all right. The old woman that was keeping them, the grandma, she's got a broken leg. The mama and daddy are at work out on the Wansley farm."

"We've got a man on the way out there now," the sheriff said. He dropped his cigarette and stepped on it. A siren began to wail far off. A squawk came from his car, and he walked toward it.

People said a woman named Amoreena Harper had predicted the tornado. She had told people at her church, Christ Chapel AME, that the town would soon be called to account for its evil ways. After the storm hopped across the community, she stood out in front of her house and shouted to the world, calling herself a prophet.

She was not alone in seeing the storm as divine retribution. A local Baptist minister, a white man who wrote a column for the newspaper, likened the town to one of the biblical cities of the plain. Though he did not name them, he made reference to two men who lived together, an interracial couple who could be seen walking down the street holding hands. He called them an abomination in the sight of the Lord, and he accused them of having brought the tornado.

For months, the local paper received letters supporting his position. The same-sex couple was reviled by some in both the white and the black communities. But the white minister had also invoked the story of Ham and the Old Testament justifications of separation of the races. Ten years earlier, his church had voted to bar all people of color from worship when a few blacks tried to attend services.

There was also a letter from the owner of the local farm equipment factory, the man rumored to be the big donor to the college. He decried the backward thinking that laid the blame for what was a natural event on others. No one is to blame, he said. It was the planet, it was just the weather.

Amoreena Harper was a small woman in her early thirties whose eyes glared and challenged and never softened. She'd lived in the town only a month when the tornado hit. People said she had come from Philadelphia, where she had been a root-worker of some kind. It was said she'd had to leave there after she put a spell on a man and caused him to burn down his own house.

## *48.*

Dr. Caruthers knew a lot about the practices of conjurers—that was the term she used—having read all of Zora Neale Hurston's research documenting those activities in different American black communities, as well as in Haiti and Jamaica. Hurston had been trained by Franz Boas, the prominent anthropologist at Columbia University.

Her research also included being partially initiated into the tradition herself, receiving instruction in New Orleans and in Haiti, where she apparently angered another practitioner and was stricken with a violent and nearly fatal intestinal illness.

One method for producing such an effect, she later reported, was to cut the hair of a horse's tail into very fine bits and to sprinkle that on someone's food, infesting it with all the germs carried by the tail. This was known to produce serious infections and intestinal sores.

Dr. Caruthers said, "There is an actual discipline, you know. There are some very specific practices, even with respect to matters that largely rest on superstition, as parts of the tradition clearly do. There is an actual pharmacology of conjure practice that's empirically based and very powerful. But this Harper woman is merely another person whose bizarre behavior has led to rumors of the occult. She's not well. I hope someone is able to help her."

For Dr. Caruthers, Zora Neale Hurston was a deep truth teller—even in her fiction, perhaps especially there—but also a very good actor, a trait helpful in conducting her folklore research. When she went into rural black areas—and this was true even near Eatonville, Florida, the all-black town where she grew up—people tended to be wary of her as an outsider with money who dressed differently and drove a fancy car and whose speech at times reflected her education, a person with whom they did not feel comfortable telling their stories or singing their songs.

"So she took on a persona. She changed her manner of dress and claimed to be a bootlegger on the run. She sat in on the storytelling sessions and offered stories of her own that others found entertaining, and in this way she found acceptance and access to the genuine material she was looking for.

"Now, it's true that she introduced fictional elements into other parts of her life as well. At the age of twenty-six, she claimed to be ten years younger in order to attend high school, a deception I have to admire. It allowed her to go on to Howard and Barnard.

"And she did marry a twenty-three-year-old when she was in her forties, claiming to be not quite thirty, as her looks allowed her to do. The marriage didn't last, though. She had to be free to travel around and do her research. She wouldn't let anything interfere with that.

"But you need to understand that Zora was absolutely committed to telling the truth in her work. She made meticulous recordings of traditional folktales and music. And she could not abide the distorting transformations that inevitably took place when the material was appropriated for presentation to white audiences."

## *49.*

Claude and Arlene had built their frame house so far out in the country, they lived on what was called a fire road, Fire Road 124. As you rounded the curve, Arlene's mural would come into view.

It was early during our first quarter, and Walt had never been to the Jacksons' house. I wanted to see his reaction to the mural, an ambiguous landscape that stretched the length of the south wall, the horizon either at dawn or sundown—you couldn't tell which, or at least I couldn't.

Walt found it remarkable. He and Arlene discussed it for quite a while that afternoon, but all he said when he first saw it was, "*That's* different."

People were in the sun room, mostly the same group as usual, and in the middle of some disagreement as we walked in.

Dr. Oliver said, "Well, she can kiss my black ass."

Camille said, "I doubt she has any interest in kissing your black ass or any other part of your black anatomy, and I don't see any need to be so hostile about it either. It's not personal, you know."

"It *is* personal. It's *very* personal. She has no respect for the black man. Did you read what she wrote?"

"I did."

"So you know what I mean."

And then no one spoke. I suspected the silence was because of Walt and me.

Dr. Mirza stood to shake Walt's hand. "I believe I've met your wife? She works in the registrar's office?"

"Yes. Yes, she does."

"She was very pleasant, very helpful."

Dr. Mirza returned to his usual seat at the end of the sofa, a can of Coke beside him. He did not drink alcohol.

## *50.*

Walt had met Lisa when he was a graduate student at Cornell, where she was getting an MBA. The college found a job for her in the registrar's office. They were a puzzle never solved. Walt was short and heavy, with ordinary looks. Lisa was much taller, with long blonde hair and a figure that drew remarks from male students when she walked across campus. I once heard someone say, "That's Dr. Bonner's wife? *Damn.*"

For the most part, Lisa kept to herself. I wondered if she felt uncomfortable at the college, but Walt said she didn't. He said she was enjoying her chance to observe the rural South, and it was mostly the white culture that intrigued her. She liked walking around the small town and listening to people and surreptitiously taking notes on a vernacular that was new to her and often amused her.

And she was clearly amused by the way *I* spoke, which sometimes bothered me. I mentioned that to Dr. Caruthers once. She, of course, was also occasionally entertained by my regional pronunciations.

She said, "I don't know if I've ever told you this, but it might give you some perspective. When Zora went to college, the other students laughed at her. Now, think about that. When she took French at Barnard, those little girls laughed at Zora Neale Hurston. They laughed at her pronunciation, or maybe it was the idea of a black southerner trying to speak French."

Lisa was not pleased that Walt and I spent so much time together. She thought my main goal in life was to work as little as possible and to consume alcohol when I could.

She believed Walt had the potential to do important scholarly research, and that I was not only an unhealthy influence but a person who was unwell and resistant to seeing it, and she feared it was risky to be my close friend.

"Seriously," Walt told me she said, "I can't even tell if there's really anybody *in* there."

I told him she might have a point.

*51.*

Walt complimented Arlene on her house, and she thanked him. She said, "We built it ourselves, you know. It's Claude's design, if you can call it that."

Claude said, "Freestyle architecture," and he laughed.

Walt asked Arlene if one of the buildings in the backyard was her studio.

"Why, yes," she said. "Would you like to see it? Do you paint?"

"I don't, but my father did. I would like to see it, very much."

They were crossing the backyard when Mrs. Reid walked in, dressed as if for church—heels, elegant gray dress, a strand of pearls. Dr. Reid stood and gave her a kiss, and she took a seat in the tall wicker chair generally reserved for her.

"Where you *been*?" Dr. Reid said.

"*I* was working. *My* job does not allow me to just take off and start drinking liquor whenever I want to."

Claude handed her the drink he'd prepared. Bourbon whiskey, straight up. "But I *will* tell you this." She took the glass from Claude. "Thank you, dear. The way this day has been? If I'd had a bottle in my desk, I just might have cracked it open. Good Lord, people, your president does not have sense enough to come in out of the driving rain."

"What has our leader done now?" asked Dr. Mirza.

"Oh, you won't believe this, but no, I suppose you will. At three o'clock on a Friday afternoon, he decides everybody is going to learn Japanese, all the faculty. I'm serious. All of you are to become fluent in Japanese. He wants to take a chunk of your faculty development money, some of your travel money too, and devote it to that. Vernon says the Japanese will be running the world in twenty years."

"I assure you," Dr. Mirza said, "I will not be learning Japanese."

"Shoot, Mirza," Claude said, "ain't *nobody* gonna learn Japanese. And you can bet your sweet ass Vernon *Stanridge* won't be learning Japanese. Give him a week, he'll be onto something else."

Mrs. Reid eyed Claude with chagrin. "Well, that's easy for you to say. You don't have to put up with him all the time. One day he wants to be a fireman, the next day he wants to be a cowboy, and it's *my* job to help him work on his plans to be a cowboy."

Mrs. Reid had a high, silvery, infectious laugh.

"A Japanese cowboy," Dr. Reid said.

People were laughing when Walt and Arlene walked back in. Dr. Plant said, "*Konnichiwa*, y'all."

Walt and Arlene were stopped for a second where they stood. Arlene said, "What's happening *here*?"

"But I'm more of a *sayonara* man myself," Dr. Reid said to Dr. Plant. "And I'll tell you *one* damn thing: Stan the Man wouldn't be *talking* this way if he'd been where *I* was in 1944. No sir. Not a chance in this world."

## *52.*

Curtis Oliver's instrument was the piano, but he could also play saxophone and guitar. He played mainly jazz, but he'd try anything. One afternoon, people started naming songs and singers and composers, and Dr. Oliver had it all. He played Debussy and Fats Waller and Chopin and Art Tatum. I said he must be some kind of musical genius, and that didn't make him happy. "Listen," he said, "I've *seen* genius and I've *heard* it. I'm a competent musician, that's all. I try my best to get it right, and I try to feel it. But I've been in the presence of Duke Ellington and Ray Charles, you understand, and Miles Davis, and so the word *genius* has a real meaning to me. I know how it moves and what it sounds like and what it can do, and believe me, I'm no genius."

*53.*

Jarvis had caught shrapnel from a mortar round that threw him twenty feet and permanently damaged his back, and he was always in some pain.

In the VA hospital he had come to feel lucky, having met so many men who wished they had died in Vietnam.

He told us about R. T. Gibson, a white man whose face had melted into frog lips and no nose and terrifying eyes, and whose skull was a plastic dome—a hero with two tours of duty, seven Air Medals, almost two hundred combat missions, three Purple Hearts, the Bronze Star.

R. T. told everybody his philosophy of survival: It was necessary to "eliminate threat at the source." He told this to anybody who came onto the ward, first thing.

Jarvis said R. T. sought him out right away. He brought his monstrous face close and rasped a whisper, which was the only way he could speak.

"If you stay back," he said, "the fear builds up. You got to go out after it and eliminate threat at the source. Do you hear what I'm telling you? You *can't* stay back. You got to go out after it."

*54.*

The booming bass hit us, and the musty burning smell. Walt stepped into the room lit mainly by the aquarium, and I followed him.

I heard Jarvis say, "What it is, doctors. What it shall be."

"Hey, you guys," Walt said, "how's it going?"

"Ain't nothing to it" came from somewhere.

"Hey there, Spaceman," Danielle said to Walt in a dreamy and mock-flirtatious voice. "Come on over here and teach me something."

He sat beside her, and I took one of the easy chairs and was handed the joint by a young man I didn't know. I inhaled and passed it to Walt, who did the same and gave it to Danielle.

Walt's eyes said he was stoned off one hit. He rarely got high, but he had a naturally spaced-out demeanor, walking across campus oblivious to whatever was not in his head, neglecting to greet people. But students who knew Walt from his classes cut him some slack. They started calling him the Spaceman.

Danielle poured the sweet wine into plastic cups and handed them to us, and the taste made everything seem right. Marvin Gaye singing "the way they do my life" seemed like an enactment of fate. My arms and legs felt exact and the space behind my eyes and up into my forehead felt loose and warm and also seemed predestined somehow to feel loose and warm.

The aquarium, about six feet from where I sat, was a box of clean light, and it resembled a shrine right then. Soon enough, that's what it would become.

Someone was still talking, but the fish were deep in a silence that had begun to matter, with their gliding ease, their eyes manifesting a purity of witness, beholding a truth that was not ours and never could be. I heard Walt say the word *contingency* and looked over and saw Danielle shaking her head no.

"Listen," Jarvis said to me, "when I got back to the world, after I got out of the hospital, I was on all kinds of chemicals the doctors gave me. I'm talking about some heavy shit. I felt like I was underwater. One day I just decided to stop. I didn't take any of the pills. I drove up to that new mall and went in the pet store and stood there looking at the fish and came back with this tank.

"Check this out: those two over there are your black mollies, and these two coming around down here are your black skirt tetras. Yeah, these are my girls, these are my babies. I take good care of them."

## *55.*

One afternoon, I found myself talking too much. Jarvis just listened. I'd rattled on for a long time, about a lot of things. I ended up talking about the people who want to be frozen and brought back to life.

"But then there you *are*," I said, "the loneliest person in the world, right? I mean, they thaw you out, and you look around and realize they're going to study you like a lab rat. *They* don't really care about you. Anybody who *did* care about you has been dead for two hundred years. And what are you going to *do*, anyhow? Sit up and have some breakfast? And what if they preserved nothing but your head? You wake up and you're nothing but a *head*? If your nose itches, you can't scratch it. What good would that be? By then surely they'd be able to attach a body onto you and wire you up, yeah, but then what would you do? You think they'd let you go home? You wouldn't *have* a home. Nobody would recognize you. Nobody would meet you on the sidewalk and ask where have you been. Everybody would be a stranger. Maybe what they need to do is have *communities* of frozen people. Freeze people *as* communities, and bring them *back* as communities, so they won't be so lonely. Now *that's* an idea. That would be a good grant proposal: 'Future Traumatic Loneliness in the Cryogenic Returnee: A Community-based Preventative.' But of course, then..."

Jarvis was laughing.

"*What*?" I asked. "What did I say?"

He put a hand over his face and shook his head and waved me away and laughed harder.

"*What*?"

Finally, he said, "Nothing really, but it's just that sometimes you get this look on your face that cracks me up. And you had it a minute ago. That's all."

"What look?"

"Forget about it, man. I'm just playing." But he couldn't stop smiling.

"Come on, now. What look?"

He took a drink of beer and sat back and lit a cigarette. Jarvis was rarely in a hurry to answer a question.

In a little while he said, "All right." He lifted the roach from the ashtray and re-lit it, took a hit and passed it to me. "It has to do with what I just put in your hand."

"What about it?"

"Look now, you know me. I get fucked up whenever I want to, but it looks like you do too. Me, I understand why, but you, I don't. You just getting high? Is that it?"

"Yeah, I guess. Why not?"

"Hold on, now," he said. "Everything's cool, everything's fine, but I mean sometimes I look at you, and you look so *serious*, and then you say something that just undercuts it. You know what I mean. We all do it sometimes, I know that. But you get that look, and I say to myself, 'Uh-oh, here it comes.' You had the look a few minutes back, and then you started in on, 'Well, if you froze your head, you'd be lonely when you woke up....'" He threw his head back and laughed and slapped the arm of the sofa.

I guess I looked bewildered. Maybe I looked mad.

"Hey, don't be so uptight, man. Look," he said, "here it is: When I'm fucked up, I *know* I'm fucked up, that's all. But it's like you *don't*. Like you believe you're thinking even *better* than before, like you fixing to *discover* something, gonna *explain* things. I get fucked up so I can see less, not more, so I can *stop* seeing things, or focus on other things, and it works pretty good. And yeah, it does make me feel good, feel high, I mean, you know, feel right, but there's a price to pay, too. Dr. Plant says I medicate myself with weed so I don't have to deal with things, and he's right, I know that. He says I ought to find another way, if I can. I know he's right about that too. Smoke enough of this shit, though, and I don't dream at all, and that's fine with me."

Smoking usually made me feel bad—anxious and suspicious without reason, and talkative in a way that I recognized as mostly nonsense but was helpless to stop. It depressed me to hear myself. I soon quit smoking altogether and stuck with my primary form of medication, which was always alcohol, usually administered late in the day, followed by fast food and a solitary evening with the TV. I discovered that whatever I did, the time would pass.

*56.*

Jarvis played chess every day, usually in the student center. Students gathered in the game room next to the snack bar to play pool and cards and chess. Gambling was not allowed, but it still went on.

Rondell Willis, also known as Gold Monkey—because of a piece of jewelry he was said to wear—had served time as a juvenile at Alto and that's where he'd learned the game. Nobody at the college could beat him—students, faculty, or staff.

Jarvis had started playing chess in Vietnam. He offered to teach me. I already played—I had a book for beginners—but over and over again, I made stupid moves. Even when I tried seriously to learn the game, I made little progress. I couldn't seem to focus, couldn't see what was right in front of me.

One day when I went to the snack bar for a sandwich, I saw Jarvis and Gold Monkey sitting in the far corner of the game room, surrounded by a few students watching in silence, which was one of the rules for chess spectators. The room was loud, the talk never stopped.

At the tables reserved for cards—usually bid whist or spades, I was told—the players challenged and goaded one another, but if you were watching a chess match, you didn't comment on the action or talk to the players or to one another; you didn't say anything at all.

On my way out, I went into the game room to see how Jarvis was doing. The room was royal blue, windows with open Venetian blinds all along one side, and the window light, as well as the fluorescent bulbs overhead and the cigarette smoke in the air, gave the room a bluish haze hard on the eyes. I walked over to the chess area. Danielle was there, and three young men I didn't know. She glanced at me, then looked hard at the board.

I moved closer to the table. Jarvis was playing white, and he had the advantage in pieces, but Gold Monkey controlled the center. I walked back to my office.

Later that day Walt and I went over to Jarvis's, and I found out he had lost again, not long after I left. I told him I'd thought he was in pretty good shape.

"Two moves away from checkmate," he said. "I could see it coming, but I couldn't get out of it."

Danielle walked in from the kitchen. "You didn't see Gold Monkey's queen?"

"I didn't."

"Man, you ain't no chess player. You half blind."

*57.*

Dr. Reid gave me a copy of his first book, *Patriotic Hypocrisy: Lynchings and the Black Veteran*. I took it to Jarvis's house to show him a passage describing an event that had taken place not far from where I knew Jarvis had grown up.

*Chicago Defender,* April 5, 1919

**Negro Veteran Lynched**
**For Refusing to Doff Uniform**

> Blakely, Ga., Apr. 4—When Private William Little, a Negro soldier returning from the war arrived at the station here several weeks ago, he encountered a band of whites who ordered him to doff his Army uniform and walk home in his underwear. Several other whites prevailed, and Little was left alone. Little continued to wear his uniform over the next few weeks, as he had no other clothing. Anonymous notes were sent him warning him not to wear his uniform "too long" and advising him to leave town if he wished to "sport around in khaki." Yesterday Private Little was found dead on the outskirts of this city, apparently beaten by a mob. He was wearing his Army uniform.

Jarvis said, "There it *is.*" He wanted to keep the book and read the whole thing. He still had it when he died.

## *58.*

Dr. Reid told me he was doing a series of interviews with the generation of white and black southerners born soon after World War II, and he asked if I would come over for dinner some evening. We could do the interview afterwards.

"Yes sir," I said. "I'd like that. I don't know that I have anything to say that would make for an interesting interview."

He said not to worry. He had a standard list of questions. "When I compare one person's answers with another's, you see, the difference can be revealing. You don't have to say anything special. Just try to tell the truth."

Dr. Reid lived in an antebellum house about three miles outside of town—a white frame house with large columns and a wrap-around porch with swings and rockers. He and his wife had bought it for almost nothing in 1965, when it had been in serious disrepair.

I arrived to find they had also invited Camille, who was working with Dr. Reid on the interview project. After an early dinner, we all moved into Dr. Reid's study, a spacious room with bookshelves that reached the high ceiling. One wall of shelves was devoted to his collection of historical documents and racist memorabilia, which was the source of a good bit of discussion at the college, and I had heard him talk about it with Camille, who wanted him to let her put some parts on display in the library's Negro Collection, which she supervised. The items were no surprise to me. I'd seen things like that all my life—I see them today—but I'd never seen such a variety, and I'd never seen so many in one place.

I picked up a document, a newspaper clipping encased in a sleeve, with this advertisement:

> Negroes for sale:<br>
> A woman and two children, 8 and 3<br>
> Together or separately Sold for Cash<br>
> or traded for groceries Several small<br>
> boys without their mothers

On the table beside me were two ashtrays. One was dusty with ash and the other seemed never to have been used. A small figurine of a naked black boy stood at its center. His skin was as black as they could make it, and his overlarge mouth's wide smile showed an unnatural number of brilliant white teeth enveloped in swollen red lips, his bulging eyes as white as his teeth.

Beside the ashtrays was an old book with note cards sticking out. Camille picked it up.

"Oh, *this* thing," she said. "I've been looking for a copy of this. Wallace Lee, did you know that?"

"That's why I put it there."

The book was *The Negroes in Negroland: The Negroes in America and Negroes Generally: Also, the several races of white men, considered as the involuntary and predestined supplanters of the black races.*

"Now, that book was written in 1868 by a man named Helper," Dr. Reid said, "and it was a very popular book at the time. Helper was a southern white man who'd been an opponent of slavery in an earlier book, one that was very controversial. He was reviled in the South, and people were lynched—I'm talking about white folks—for just owning the book.

"He argued against slavery because he thought it kept ordinary whites in poverty, since there was no way for them to compete with the labor of slaves. But when the slaves were freed, Helper came out like a wild man against any kind of equal treatment. Now *this* would be a real psychological case study for you, doctor. In his later books this man proposed the extermination of *all* people of color."

Dr. Reid asked for the book. "Let me read you something that will show the pathological and cruel edge to this man's thinking, if you can call it thinking, and how unbalanced his perceptions are by his own venom. There is truly a kind of poison in the words he comes up with to describe this creature whom he detests, but who does not, in fact, exist."

He read aloud in his deep bass: "In addition to the black and baneful color of the negro, there are numerous other defects, physical, mental, and moral, which clearly mark him, when compared with the white man, as a very different and inferior creature. Let us, also, at the same time, take cognizance of His low and compressed Forehead; His hard, thick Skull; His small, backward-thrown Brain; His short, crisp Hair; His flat Nose; His thick Lips; His projecting, snout-like Mouth; His strange, Eunuch-toned Voice; The scantiness of Beard on his Face ; The Toughness and Unsensitiveness of his Skin; The Thinness and Shrunkenness of his Thighs; His curved Knees; His calfless Legs; His low, short Ankles; His long, flat Heels; His glut-shaped Feet; The general Angularity and Oddity of his Frame; The Malodorous Exhalations from his Person; His Puerility of Mind; His Inertia and Sleepy-headedness; His proverbial Dishonesty; His predisposition to fabricate Falsehoods...."

"Wallace Lee," Mrs. Reid said, "you can stop it now. Your eunuch-toned voice is depressing me."

Camille said, "Not to mention the thinness and shrunkenness of your thighs."

"Hold on now, little lady," Dr. Reid said. "You don't know nothing *about* my thighs. You'd be better off going with this 'predisposition to fabricate falsehoods,' since in my case, that has some truth to it."

Mrs. Reid said, "Indeed it does."

"Now Everett," Dr. Reid said, "I shared this with you partly because I have a question for you to consider. I'm wondering how a performance like this leaves you *feeling*. You can see clearly how much fun this man was having. He was wound up, wasn't he? I'm sure he was mighty pleased with himself.

"Now, what I'd like to know about that passage is this: when you listen to it, do you ever find yourself being *entertained* by it? That's what all this is *for*, you know"—he swept a hand toward the shelves of memorabilia—"the enjoyment and entertainment of white folks. Do you ever find yourself unable to resist a kind of seemingly involuntary pleasure, similar to what one might experience with pornography, for example? My guess is that you do, but of course, I don't know that."

He didn't wait for an answer. "Well, let's get to work," he said. "First thing we want to do is get some basic biographical information on you. We've got this standard form"—Camille gave me a single sheet of paper—"so if you'll just take a minute to fill it out."

The questions were the usual ones: birthplace, family, education, employment, affiliations. I completed the form and handed it to Camille, who set it aside.

Mrs. Reid stepped to the window and opened the curtain to reveal a flower garden and beyond that, a small pond that caught the setting sun. From where I sat, the water was a spangled and shifting darkness. On the other side of the pond, a pecan orchard lined its way toward the horizon, the trees fixed in their strict geometry of shade.

Dr. Reid said, "Okay, let's start out with your hometown, let's talk about Monroe a little bit. What kind of a place is it? I know it's small, about ten or eleven thousand, right? How do people make a living there?"

I said there were cotton farms and dairy farms and chicken farms, two cotton mills, a cotton gin, a poultry processor, a place that sewed blue jeans.

"Okay, that's good. If we need more, we can get the data from public records. What about churches? Did you and your family go to church?"

"Our grandparents went to a Baptist church a few miles out of town, a country church they belonged to all their lives, and when we went to church, that's where we went."

The sun had gone under with unusual quickness, it seemed, and now the pond was barely visible, as if the landscape were drifting to sleep. I took a sip of the cognac Mrs. Reid had brought me.

"What would you like us to know about your parents?" Camille asked.

I said my father had left us when we were small, so I couldn't say much about him. My mother had serious health problems and didn't live at home for long periods.

"What kind of health problems did she have?"

I didn't go into detail. I said she'd been emotionally unwell. They didn't pursue it further. I told them she'd died of breast cancer when I was a junior in college.

"I'm so sorry to hear that," Camille said. "That must have been very hard for you and your brother."

"Yes, I'm sure it was," Mrs. Reid said.

We sat there for a little while, nobody saying anything, as though we were observing a moment of silence for my mother.

"I suppose we should ask about the schools," Camille finally said. "Were they good? Did you go to public school?"

"That's the only kind we had, until I was a junior in high school, when four black girls came to our school, and some people began to organize a private Christian academy."

"How did your grandparents feel about that?"

"They never said much about it, but I know they thought integration would never work, and that there would need to be private schools. They didn't think white people would ever get used to having their children go to school with black children."

Mrs. Reid said, "Do you think that's how most of the white townspeople felt?"

"Yes, ma'am."

"And why do you think that was?"

"What was?"

"Why do you think they felt that way? Why did the town believe white folks could never get used to integration?"

Her question stopped me. She knew the answer. Did she just want to hear me say the words? By this time, it was completely dark. Anyone out in the garden would have been invisible to me, but they would have been able to see me clearly.

## *59.*

Isaac Bell was one of my advisees. When I called him Mr. Bell, he said he preferred Isaac. It wasn't because he wanted to be on familiar terms, but because he disliked his last name and the man who had given it to him.

"Isaac, then. Is it Ike?"

"Ain't no Ike in the Bible. Just Isaac. I got a brother named Jacob and a sister named Naomi, all names my mother chose."

Isaac had lost his legs in a railroad accident when he was twenty-three. He was twenty-eight when I met him. He'd been throwing switches on the tracks when his foot got stuck, and he was caught between two freight cars and essentially cut in half, the tip of his spine crushed. He'd had a wife and a daughter, but after his injury, his wife left him and went to Baltimore and took the girl with her.

Isaac had been born again in a new body electrified by nightmare pain. He took prescribed narcotics every day, though he had gone for excruciating stretches trying not to.

"Doc, let me tell you something," he said one day. "I've been awake five nights straight. That's no lie."

He was always in pain, even with the morphine. In his first years after the injury, he had taken all kinds of drugs on top of it. He'd almost died after taking too many Quaaludes.

"You see all these Negroes acting up in the street, out of their heads?" he said to me. "I had them all beat. I *did.*"

A divine hand had gripped his foot and set the car rolling—that's what he'd come to believe—and the purpose of his life now was to learn how to surrender to the will of God. Isaac had a laugh that bubbled up from deep in his chest. He would roll into my office singing a hymn, a witness for Jesus, though he did not feel compelled to preach. His witness was one of prayer. Of song too, but mainly prayer.

"I trust in Christ Jesus," he said. "I do what Paul told the Thessalonians to do. I pray without ceasing. Doc, I look at it this way. If I see that you are lost—and I do see it, you know, I see it clear as day—I can preach to you and I can argue with you and I can witness.

"I can do that, and it is what the Bible tells us to do, you know, in Matthew the twenty-eighth chapter, verses nineteen and twenty. Look it up. But what I believe in is prayer. I believe that if I call on the Lord for your sake, he'll reach you in ways my words never could. The Lord will make something happen, that's what I believe. It's up to you to pay attention, so you don't miss it."

*60.*

In *The Varieties of Religious Experience,* William James writes:

> "There is a certain uniform deliverance in which religions all appear to meet:
>
> Two parts. An uneasiness and its solution. The uneasiness, reduced to its simplest terms, is a sense that there is something wrong about us as we naturally stand.
>
> The solution is a sense that we are saved from the wrongness by making proper connection with the higher powers."

*61.*

I played three games for the faculty team, but my knee gave out. My last game was against the students of Omega Psi Phi. The Ques had two former varsity players who'd used up their eligibility but were still in school—Damon Respress, the 6'9" power forward who'd been all-conference, and Avery Whitaker, the 5'11" point guard who had been the team leader in assists and in free-throw percentage.

He was a slash-to-the-basket kind of player, fearless going into the lane against big men. Years later, when I saw Allen Iversen play, I thought about Avery Whitaker.

Claude was our point guard and team captain. He'd played basketball in high school, and at Tuskegee he had run the 440. Daniel Carney played, and Snake Underwood, Gerard Fulton, and Horace Dukes, and a few more people, and of course Vernon Stanridge, who always started and demanded to play center.

The team humored him, since he had no stamina and was never in the game but a few minutes. He'd post up with his back to the basket and shoot hook shots. If the ball went to Stan the Man, you could tell it goodbye. People joked that he didn't shoot a sky hook, but a bye hook.

The Ques blew us out of the gym, but not before Claude stole the ball twice from Avery Whitaker. The second time it happened, the look on Whitaker's face cracked everybody up. Claude was an amazing athlete. He was forty-seven years old.

## *62.*

Isaac Bell and Camille Williams were first cousins, as I discovered when he called her from my office one day, and she came over to give him a ride.

She knocked on the open door. Isaac said, "Miss Librarian. How you doing?"

She leaned down and kissed him on top of his head. “I’m doing well, Jet. Doing well. Is this man treating you right?”

“He’s trying, I give him that, he’s trying, but he needs to open up his mind. That’s what I think.”

“He’s got too many questions I can’t answer,” I said.

“What kind of questions?”

“All kinds, but we don’t want to get into it now, do we?”

Isaac said, “Why not?”

“I guess I thought y’all were about to leave. I imagine Miss Williams needs to get back to the library.”

“No, I’m done for the day.”

“What name did you call Isaac?”

“Oh, I called him Jet. That’s what people used to call him when he was a boy, before he got to be an old man.”

“Look here,” he said. “Who’s the oldest?”

“You’re still an old man.” She nudged his wheelchair with her knee.

“She’s got me by three years, Doc.”

“So y’all are cousins?”

“First cousins. I been knowing this little old lady all my life.”

He looked up at her, and she smiled at him, and it was the only time I had seen such joy in her eyes.

“Doc and me were talking about that old problem of the body and the mind, and the body and the soul, and the soul and the mind—all that, you know—and about how everything is mixed in and how everything fits together.”

“And did you get it cleared up?”

“Got it all settled, yes we did, yes we did. And he’s still wrong. Doc’s got a mighty hard head on him.”

As they left, I noticed she didn't touch his chair—he'd had some trouble turning it around—and I remembered how, when he and I went down the hall to the vending machines last week, I started to push him and he told me not do that.

After class one day, Isaac handed me a manila folder. "My cousin probably didn't tell you she wrote poems, did she?"

I said I'd heard she was supposed to be a poet.

"Yeah, but you don't want to call her that. She won't like it. She says she can do without folks who want everybody to know they're poets. She knows a woman who put 'Poet' on her license plate. She can't stand that kind of thing. I don't really know what her problem is. But look here, I got a few poems from the book she's trying to write. She calls it *Bootleg Yesterday* for some reason. Don't ask me why. She won't let anybody read it. But I got my hands on this, a few pages. I thought you might like to see it."

I took the folder and laid it on my desk and said I'd give it a look. I was headed to a meeting. I didn't tell him I was not likely to read poetry, which usually confused and irritated me, and still does, for the most part. Later, I opened the folder and saw a poem entitled "Let Mr. Charles Try To Explain," but I didn't read it.

*63.*

Yusef Ishmael had graduated in 1968, but he was still on campus. He had taken that name and adopted parts of the ideology of Elijah Muhammad, though he did not wear the suit and bow tie of the Fruit of Islam. He had Pan-African interests. He dressed in flowing, colorful clothes—dashiki, kufi, and sandals. He wore a large wooden Africa-shaped medallion painted red, green, and black. I saw him in the student center every day, talking intensely with students, and he would wave me over and engage me in what, it became clear, was a ritual of some kind.

"Let me ask you this, doctor," he said. "Back in the day, if you needed to *buy* a person—you know, maybe you had sold somebody or somebody had died or run off, or maybe you accidentally horsewhipped somebody to death, and you had to *restock,* for whatever reason—out of the two of us, me and Malik here, which one would you have bought? Now, I'm better *looking* than Malik, that's obvious, anybody can see that, but he's stronger. Feel his arm. Go on, feel it. Don't want to? But that's not the real question. What we want to know is, for either one of us, what do you think a fair price would be in *today's* market?"

One day he said, "Listen, we're having a disagreement, and we need you to settle it for us because we think you'll probably know the answer. The question is this: How much wood would a peckerwood peck if a peckerwood *could* peck wood?"

He always waited for a response, and he never owned up to the joke in his question, if joke is the right word. He chose to be cordial, but he let me know he never forgot who I was. He thought I was the Devil. He'd made that very clear to me, and he didn't think there was anything I could do about it either. What was, was. What was done, was done.

He liked to say, "Ain't history a bitch?"

He asked for my thoughts about his proposal to place a statue on the quad to honor a white man. "It'll be like that statue they have out in Louisiana, the one they call Uncle Jack, The Good Darkey. You know the one I'm talking about, right?

"He's sort of bent over, you know, got his hat in his hand? We don't have the name yet. Ours will be making some kind of gesture, but we don't know what he'll be doing." He asked for my opinion about the name.

"I guess I don't have one," I said.

"Don't have one. All right, then. We might just name it after you, so you try to figure out what you want to be doing."

One day when he called me over, he was sitting with a group of students. Jamal Malik was one of them.

"Where you headed?"

"Going to class," I said. "I'm late already."

"Listen," he said, "I've got a serious question for you. Have you ever heard of what they call the convict lease system? Do you know what that is?"

"I'm not sure."

"Come on, now. The convict lease system. Black prisoners being loaned out to white farmers to work on their land. Malik was in a class where the term came up, the convict lease. Do you know about that, or have you ever heard of people doing that?"

I said I hadn't.

"See now," he said, "that's hard for me to believe. I think you *have* to know. That was the question that came up in Reid's history class. He said white folks don't know their own history, don't even know about the things they've done to black people. Like the convict lease system. He said most white folks don't even know about that, but I say that's just another lie. Y'all do know, you have to know."

I said I didn't.

Jamal Malik let loose a dismissive hiss.

"All right, then," Yusef Ishmael said, "I'll tell you a story from my own family, so you try to listen, all right? Try hard now, professor. Pay close attention.

"You see, my granddaddy went to prison when my father was six years old. That's not unusual, is it? Black man goes to jail, children are raised by their mother. That's what happens.

"But my granddaddy went to jail, went to prison—where he died, where they worked him to death—for walking down the road. You believe that? His crime was walking down the road. White folks want to say, well, he must have done more than that, he had to have done more than that, you don't arrest a man for walking down the road. Tell me this, professor: what good is your life if you can't even walk down the road? And this was a *righteous* man, a deacon in the church, just walking down the road. A man who did not curse or drink alcohol, who taught his children right from wrong, and all he was doing was walking down the road. This was a man who worked hard doing whatever job he could find, usually farm work, picking cotton, plowing behind somebody else's mule. And he was a fair carpenter. He did whatever he could do to feed his family and put clothes on their backs. He paid his bills, and was respectful to white people. He was not what y'all like to call uppity. He acted like he knew his place. And where did all that get him? *Y'all* arrested him for walking to *work*, walking up to the cotton gin in town to help build a platform, about a three-mile walk. Arrested him for not having proof of employment on him. No papers to prove he had a job.

"Now, he *had* a job, he had more than *one* job, but he didn't have any papers on him to prove it. He told the sheriff who to talk to, but it didn't matter. Y'all needed somebody, and he was it. Took him in for vagrancy, locked him up and leased him out to farmers, transferred him to the state prison, in the same kind of deal, and that's where he died. We never knew exactly how. Y'all would even talk to anybody. *That's* the convict lease system, but it's just another kind of slavery, that's all it is. Now, are you gonna stand there and try to say you never *heard* about it?"

"Well, I never did," I said. "Believe what you want to, but look, I've got to go."

"You sure as hell do."

*64.*

Jarvis and I were watching the game. There was a vicious hit, and a man lay motionless on the field. The player who had made the hit waved frantically to the sidelines for help. The crowd fell silent. The announcers kept talking.

The player was badly hurt, and the delay stretched out as the medical personnel prepared him to be moved. Just before the commercial, the announcers, in reverential tones, told us the player's hobbies.

When Jarvis looked at me, it was like somebody had slapped him in the face for no reason.

"The boy may be paralyzed for life—we don't know—and they talking about how much he loves to *water ski*? They just need to stop talking."

The player was loaded onto the transport cart, which began to make its way toward the gate at the end of the field—slowly and steadily, as if pulled by a cord. The crowd gave that show of support which is always cut with anxious hesitation. Sometimes the injured player will raise an arm to the crowd, and then the applause will change tone and grow brighter, mixed with shouts and whoops.

But that afternoon, no such moment made things easier. The player rode into the dark tunnel lying as still as a dead man ferried toward an underworld, and there was a kind of flat lamentation in the applause that arose in the stadium.

Jarvis went to the hospital one night—for what turned out to be food poisoning—where he was treated by a nurse, a white woman named Nicole who had recently moved from Atlanta. She was thirty-three, six years older than Jarvis. They started going out. Eventually, I would see pictures of her—she had short blonde hair—but I never saw her in person.

*65.*

Dr. Plant and I were in Dr. Reid's office discussing the upcoming accreditation visit and reviewing our lists of goals and objectives and implementation strategies and milestones and assessment methods.

It was late. Most people had gone home, only a few students around. Mrs. Wells always worked late, but she was setting things in order to leave.

"Man, I tell you," Dr. Reid said. "All this? This is *not* what I signed up to do. Try to solve these little puzzles about how to prove we did this and prove we did that. Covered this, improved on that, demonstrated such and such. Reached seventy percent mastery on something that matters this year because somebody somewhere decided it does, but that you know damn well won't matter next year, because somebody else will be saying it doesn't. I'm sick of it."

That was his opinion, yet he was the chair of the university committee on accreditation, and he was doing what had to be done, as well as making sure others did so too.

Dr. Plant said, "Got to be accountable to the taxpayer, Doc, you know that."

"I've been accountable all my life. Look here, Twin, people act like they are *the* taxpayer. I was paying *my* taxes back when my little Esmeralda was going down here to Burns Elementary and studying mathematics out of secondhand textbooks from the white school across town. Was I *the* taxpayer then, and if not, why not? That was my tax money they were spending on those new books that were too good for my little girl. Who was accountable to *me*?

"Look, I'm just very tired. I know the answer, and I know what we need to do for this accreditation too, and we'll do it. It's got to be done, and we'll do it, and we'll do it right. But all this righteous talk gets to me sometimes, I swear to God, it really does."

At the end of our eighth-grade year, we found out the class after ours would be getting new English textbooks, and the ones we'd been using would be given to Carver.

I sat behind a boy who filled his book with racial slurs and drawings that depicted blacks as apes and put black girls in sexual poses with white boys. He drew well, he had talent. He made you see it.

*66.*

Claude's master's degree was in physical education—he could be seen running his five miles around the campus perimeter every day—but he had majored in philosophy as an undergraduate, and he taught a philosophy class as well.

During his early hospitalizations—for manic-depression, the same diagnosis as my mother's, though her condition was much worse—and during his periods of trying to heal, he had read philosophy books, to which he gave some credit for his recoveries.

I was told that as the ten-year accreditation approached, the college would limit him to teaching PE, but after the accreditation had been reestablished, they'd give him back the philosophy class.

Isaac Bell said, "If you sit in that man's class, you end up thinking about things you never thought about before. Now don't get me wrong: he's a lost soul. But when he gets fired up in that classroom, he'll turn your head around. That's no lie. He'll do it."

*67.*

Walt was eight years old when his mother took him out of

school and said they were going to see a friend. As they approached the house, she pulled the car over and told him his father had died. She didn't say how. But Walt would grow up knowing his father had died a ridiculous death, a tragedy with slapstick built into it.

He was walking across a field behind their house when he bent down to pick up something. As he did, he took a hard step forward. His foot landed on the tines of a garden rake hidden in the tall grass, and it raised up and struck him on the forehead. A neighbor saw it happen and let go an initial laugh, but then ran to see about him. Over the years, Walt said, it had come to seem like his father had died in a cartoon.

Near the heart of Walt's emotional life was a sense of the absurd. He studied the literature of the absurd and had written his dissertation on *The Myth of Sisyphus*.

And partly because the preacher at his father's funeral had delivered a blistering sermon on heaven and hell, traumatizing the bereaved boy even further, all his life Walt had also been haunted by, and focused on, the question of the soul.

He had come to believe that the soul—conceived of as an immortal, eternally transcendent thing—was a fiction, but that it does exist as an entity made up of one's whole life and history, created and given shape inside and outside, formed by what the person becomes, by how they live, the choices they have made, by the work they do, by what their life means in the lives of others, and by what is still alive for a while inside those others and out in the world when the person is gone.

The soul is mortal, he believed, but it does exist and it moves through the world and carries an ultimate meaning. It is singular in the human universe, common to us all, and always holy.

*68.*

One afternoon at about four-thirty, I found myself clowning my way into Walt's office, doing a little rolling strut. I heard Claude say, "It breaks my heart to see her like this."

I heard him clearly. I had taken two shots of tequila from the bottle in my desk. I slid on in anyhow and interrupted him with "What's shaking, what's baking? Que pasa, big papa?" and a sickening awareness came over me, and I turned around and left.

Not long after, I went to Claude's office to apologize. We talked for a good while then—the only long conversation we ever had—and he told me things about his life that he apparently wanted me to know.

"This was before I met Arlene. I was twenty-two years old. I had driven to a high school football game up near Macon, and I was staying at a friend's place. We started drinking after the game, and we blew some of that herb that the young folks seem to think they discovered, and then my friend told me that he had cut it with something. He wasn't exactly sure what. Somebody gave it to him, and he put it on the weed. I never would have smoked it if I'd known he had cut it with something, but it was too late. I ended up running down the highway without a stitch of clothes on, on a cold night. I was *doing* that, and I was *watching* myself do it too."

"They put me in jail and then in the hospital up in Milledgeville, with about twelve thousand other people, the largest place like that in the country then. I had already been there one time before, from an episode that occurred on its own, without any help from me. I swore I would never go back to that place. And there I was again."

I knew about Central State Hospital. My mother had spent most of her adult life there. It was a monstrous place. A repository of infinite sadness.

"I sort of woke up, sort of came back to myself, in a room maybe eight by ten, nobody else in there. The cell was pitch black. You couldn't see your hand in front of your face. I felt my way around and realized there was shit on the wall, and I had stuck my hand in it. Naked and cold in the dark, shit on my hands and no way to get it off. This time I swore that if I couldn't get well, and if I had to stay in a place like that, I would find a way to stop living. But I was not in control. Nobody was going to let me make a decision about anything.

"The next day, they hosed me down and put a gown on me and strapped me to a gurney and wheeled me down the hall for a shock treatment. Back then, it didn't much matter what was wrong with you, they'd light you up.

"And when my aunt got me out of that place, after I'd had maybe five shock treatments, I didn't feel human. My mind was half erased. She tried to take care of me by herself, but she didn't know what to do. She had a little money, and she tried to get me into a good private facility, but everything was whites only, so she watched over me herself and fed me and let me sleep and rest. And that's when I read some things that helped me keep on living."

I waited for him to tell me what it was that he had read, but he didn't, so I asked him.

He said, "Well, if you want to know, I'll tell you. But I generally don't go around telling people that I read something that saved my life. It feels too much like I'm saying 'Here, read this and it'll do the same for you,' and I'm not saying that. I'm not saying it holds any universal truth either, just that, at a particular time in my life, it helped me. I was talking with your running buddy about this very thing when you came into his office acting the fool. He has read some of the same things."

They had been discussing Albert Camus and the essay in which he argues that "It is essential to die unreconciled, and not of one's own free will."

"I believe he kept me alive. I do. Now, to some folks, maybe to everybody, that makes me a cliche. They'll give me a little smile of understanding, as if to say, 'Yes, we all went through that phase.' It's like a pat on the head. Well, let me tell you. People can smile all they want. They can do a little dance while they're at it, for all I care. You can smile at anything. People smile at the Bible. Now, the Bible doesn't speak to me the way it does to some people, but I don't try to smile it away.

"This thing Arlene is going through...some days..."—his voice went hoarse; he waited— "some days, I realize she's not going to make it. But I've seen her sit there with her Bible when she was in bad pain, I've seen her lost in the Bible for a long time, and I have seen her look up a changed woman. Not just different, but changed. I've seen it in her eyes, and I've heard it in her voice.

"Now, whatever is going on there, it's not for me to tear down, it's not for me to question or diminish—and certainly not to mock—just because it doesn't speak to me the same way. If there's one thing I do know, Everett, it's that we will *all* be humbled."

I nodded, empty-headed, and I didn't ask him—how is that possible?—what Arlene was going through.

*69.*

A month before he died of a heart attack, my grandfather and I were sitting by the window at the kitchen table, both reading the newspaper.

It was a Saturday morning, two days after the final in my elementary philosophy class, my first quarter of college, and I was puffed up with the standard proofs for and against the existence of God, and I made him listen to them.

I found myself talking to him in a dismissive and abrupt way, never really thinking about what I was doing, showing off by attacking what I assumed to be his belief in an afterlife, though I had never heard him say a word about it.

He had dropped out of eighth grade after his father died and the family needed him on the farm. He was not an educated man. All he knew was the Bible. He cited John 14:2. "Jesus told us that 'In my Father's house are many mansions. If it were not so, I would have told you. I go to prepare a place for you.'"

The only way he could answer my arguments was by quoting scripture, but since he assumed the truth of scripture, he had made the error of begging the question, and I was eager to let him know that.

There was a winter bleakness to the sky above the tree line, a soiled white in a hazy drift. He was quiet, and when he finally spoke, an awful sadness had come into his voice.

"It sounds like you learned a lot, and I'm proud of you, I am. I want you to know that. If I'm telling the truth, you know, maybe I don't really think there's a heaven. If I'm telling you the straight truth from my heart, I probably don't think there is. I wish there was, though."

I was shamed to the bone that he had spoken those words because of me, a vain and foolish creature who did not know the first goddamned thing.

This was a man who prayed on his knees in his bedroom, never prayed in public, never spoke the blessing aloud at home. We always bowed our heads in silence, or maybe somebody else would say it, and he was fine with that. I never heard him tell anybody else what they ought to believe.

Donnie and Charlotte are members at Jack's Creek Baptist Church, a few miles outside town. The small wooden building has been replaced by a brick structure with the unfortunate look of a compound. But the old part of the graveyard looks the same. The day they buried Leon, Jr., there must have been two hundred people here. Three in the afternoon, the last day of July, 1966, ninety-eight degrees, the flowered air cooking under the sun into a cloying and suffocating sweetness that gave the heat an evil smell. From under the canopy came the sounds of people suffering as if they were being beaten with fists, a beating that went on and on, with no explanation and no mercy.

*70.*

West on the highway, then left where the road angles past the old hospital, now a ruin half-buried in vines, windows gone or covered with plywood. I park beside the road, near a driveway barely visible and closed off, a chain strung between two metal posts, on each post a No Trespassing sign. I step over the chain and walk up the overgrown path to the hospital steps. There's fire damage. The plywood over the front door is covered with spray paint, markings that I take to mean something, but I can't begin to understand them. This was the county's only hospital for over half a century. Donnie and I were born here, and this is where Leon died, or where he was pronounced dead. So many stories played out here, but they are nowhere in evidence. If there's history in a place like this, we bring it with us, I guess, and we carry it away. These days, more and more, I see shrines by the side of the road, marking a wreck and the death of a loved one.

*71.*

The night before the accident that killed her brother, Suzanne and I went out to Dwayne Howard's cabin, which was not much more than a shack—three rooms with musty furniture—but it was our place.

Dwayne had been inviting people to the cabin for our high school graduation parties. He'd had a string of them, all through June and July. You could show up there almost any night and find somebody. Some people went out there to drink, but Suzanne and I were not drinkers. We had taken an occasional drink, but rarely.

Dwayne locked the cabin, but he let everybody know where he'd hidden the key, and so we all thought of the place as ours. It sat beside a pond that covered maybe three acres.

That last night, when Suzanne and I first drove up, the house was dark, and we thought nobody else was there. When we got out of the car, we saw Dwayne's truck and heard "Sleepwalk" coming from inside the house—a slow song that was part of our history, always played at our high school dances, several times during the evening. I had told Suzanne I was a sleepwalker, and sometimes on the dance floor she would tease me and ask if I was awake. And I thought I was. I thought I was. I really did.

We walked onto the dock and sat at the end, under a sky lit blue by the stars, and the world held still as if caught in a photograph, until she cast a flashlight beam out over the water, into the future and the past all at once.

*72.*

Late the next afternoon, I gave Leon a ride to his girlfriend's house. She was a student at Morgan County High School, and she lived near Hard Labor Creek. Leon knew a shortcut.

We were heading into the low sun. I drove over a hill, the dirt road curved right, I hit soft sand and overcorrected, the Corvair swerved halfway into the ditch and came out and I braked too hard and we rolled.

When the doctor told me Leon had died, I faked being stricken deaf and mute, dazed and uncomprehending. I felt like an actor on stage but like someone in the audience too, as though I'd been knocked sideways but had also taken that step on purpose. Everyone saw the performance, but no one bought it.

Suzanne couldn't tolerate being anywhere near me.

Three weeks after the wreck, she went off to college, and so did I. That September, I wrote her a letter, and I wrote one to her parents, but no one answered, and after that I left them alone.

*73.*

The University of Georgia was large enough that nobody knew who I was, or cared. I had to stay on campus my freshman year, but from then on I lived alone in the old Henrietta Apartments.

I did see some people from Monroe now and then, but I tried to avoid them. I went to classes and to the library, played basketball at Stegeman Hall, picked up something from the Varsity and came home and studied and took tests and passed them. They weren't that hard. Watched TV. Went to my night job at the Bulldog Inn. Drank a lot.

That first year, when living on campus was mandatory, I had a roommate from Newark, New Jersey. His name was Harvey, but he'd been called Bucky all his life. Bucky had definite ideas about what college was for: parties and beer. He was impressively smart and had no trouble passing his classes, which he seemed to consider distractions.

We drank beer at Allen's every afternoon. He said we had to. He said we wouldn't really be in college if we didn't drink beer as much as possible. This was our time to do it. Bucky had money and a fake ID, and at four-thirty every day, he started buying pitchers, for whoever was at the table.

I didn't much like beer, but I drank it. Sometimes he'd buy whiskey from a liquor store, and I did develop a taste for that.

After I got the job as night clerk at the Bulldog Inn, three weeks into the quarter, I rarely slept in the dorm. But before I took the job, one night Bucky woke me up. He asked me what was wrong with me. I'd been crying in my sleep, he said. "You were crying hard. You don't remember? You're freaking me out, man."

It happened again the next night, and then again, and then Bucky told me I needed to make it stop, or one of us would have to go. "I can't stand listening to this."

At first, I thought there was nothing to be done, but I soon discovered I was wrong. Alcohol, consumed in sufficient quantity, proved to be a powerful dream-killer and producer of oblivion, and alcohol gave me something to hope for.

## *74.*

I've seen many accounts of slow-motion trauma, in which the event is slowed down and offered up cinematically for inspection, to be witnessed with great clarity, in fine and exquisite detail. That didn't happen to me. The wreck took place in the normal awful time it takes to roll a car. No slow, luminous particulars, no floating in suspension, able to study what might be recollected in amazement later on. I sat there covered with glass and dirt, gripping the steering wheel, the car lodged in the ditch, the windshield gone, a driveway of deep ruts nearby, my whole body pressured in an odd, underwater way and I looked at the right seat where Leon was not and failed to see his absence, and when I did, the question that came to me was an imbecile's question: How did he get out so fast? I opened the door and saw him lying in the dirt. I turned his head and dark blood trickled from his mouth onto the road and made a special kind of mud. I tried to clear his airway. His forehead was swollen and turning purple. He was breathing but sounded bad. A very old man and woman appeared at the end of the driveway. I said I needed to use their telephone. They didn't have a phone. I needed to use their car. They didn't have a car. Did anybody live nearby who had a phone? Vacant looks at each other. The woman: "They might have one over at the Maddox's place. You go down here a ways"—she pointed with her knuckle—"you take your left and you go a pretty good ways and then go across the creek and take a right, I believe. They might have one." She turned back to the man. "Does Oscar Maddox have a phone?" "There's some colored folks live not too far back that way yonder," he said. He pointed in the opposite direction. Did they have a phone? "No, they ain't never had a telephone." I told them to go in the house and get a blanket for Leon, and to bring a cool cloth, maybe some ice, and put it on his forehead and wash his face and try to keep his airway open, and try to take care of him the best they could, try to talk to him and tell him help was on the way. I took off my shirt and put it under his head and started running toward where that phone might be. I looked back and saw the woman struggling up the driveway and the old man pissing in the ditch just this side of Leon. I almost turned back. But then I ran a crazy sprint, ran as hard as I could for as long as I could, and a true question of the spirit came upon me then: who would I be if I slowed down while Leon was dying? I prayed a wild prayer. I prayed for a Biblical strength. I prayed for deliverance. An ungodly hill rose in front of me. I realized I hadn't asked the old man if the colored folks he had said lived not too far back that way yonder owned a car. My legs slowed, and slowed, and slowed. I fought to go on and fell and got up and made it to the top, where the road leveled off and went straight and seemed to run all the way to the horizon, nothing to see but more road, no turn, no driveway, no break in the ditch. Somewhere on that stretch, my legs cramped—I never found the house—and I knew Leon was dead, I knew I should have stayed there with him and tried to keep him alive. At the hospital, Suzanne came after me with her fists, hit me in the face and the throat and the stomach, hit me anywhere she could manage, shrieking at me to go away, and that's what I did.

*75.*

I have a recurring dream of being in hell. I've had it for years. I'm walking in a city. I go down a flight of stairs, as if entering a subway, and I find myself in a long corridor lined with portraits that liquefy and reshape themselves when I look at them, become the faces of human birds, menacing and grotesque. They screech and caw. I turn around to go back up the stairs, but hell has me in its undertow. The only way I can escape is if my son or daughter rescues me. I run past the squawking beaked faces, looking everywhere for some sign of my children, knowing I have no children. But then I see my daughter, and this daughter I can see only in my recurring dream is not some abstraction, she is not some idea. She's a girl about eight years old, and she looks like someone I know, she looks like her mother, someone whose name I can't call. She is my only hope, and I wake up as terrified and as lonely as I have ever been, but amazed by the girl's return—always the same girl—at the top of the stairs.

76.

William James's description of his breakdown: "There fell upon me without any warning, just as if it came out of the darkness, a horrible fear of my own existence. Simultaneously there arose in my mind the image of an epileptic patient whom I had seen in the asylum, a black-haired youth with greenish skin, entirely idiotic, who used to sit all day on one of the benches, or rather shelves against the wall, with his knees drawn up against his chin, and the coarse gray undershirt, which was his only garment, drawn over them enclosing his entire figure. He sat there like a sort of sculptured Egyptian cat or Peruvian mummy, moving nothing but his black eyes and looking absolutely nonhuman.... That shape am I, I felt, potentially. Nothing that I possess can defend me against that fate, if the hour for it should strike for me as it struck for him."

77.

Notes on the strange condition of anosognosia, the inability to acknowledge or recognize a deficit in oneself, present in different kinds of disorders

—some forms it takes:

—sensory neglect; a person may no longer attend to one side of the body, may take care of it no longer, comb the hair on one side only, brush the teeth on one side.

—a rare form of aphasia called jargon aphasia: the speaker seems unaware of, and undisturbed by, his disordered speech.

—Example: Kinsbourne and Warrington "Jargon Aphasia," *Neuropsychologia*, *1*, 27–37 (1963) "Gossiping O.K. and Lords and cricket and England and Scotland battles. I don't know. Hypertension and two won cricket, bowling, batting, and catch, poor old things, cancellations maybe gossiping, cancellations, arm and argument, finishing bowling."

—another form of anosognosia: the confabulation that can follow memory loss in Korsakoff's syndrome, a result of severe alcoholism. The person speaks fiction, but believes it's the truth.

—in very rare cases there is a form of anosognosia called Anton's syndrome or blindness denial, in which a person has gone blind but does not notice it.

*78.*

Everything from the last box has gone into the trash. I'm opening another one when Donnie shows up. He takes a Sprite out of the refrigerator and pops it open. He sits on the bed and props himself against the headboard and picks up one of the medicine bottles from the nightstand.

"Do not operate heavy machinery." He laughs his wheezy laugh. "Lay off that back-hoe, professor." He puts the bottle back on the nightstand. "Hey, you want to go out and get us something to eat? I'm kind of hungry. Maybe get us a waffle?"

There's a pain behind my eyes, and I'm a little dizzy.

"But if you don't feel up to it...."

"Yeah, I guess I don't."

A door slams, and a man and woman start to argue in Spanish. Their voices recede as they walk down the hall, their anger seems to grow, and then they are gone.

"Real reason I came over," he says, "is that I saw Suzanne Hartley at church yesterday. Not Hartley, but you know. She was at church yesterday. She's in town to deal with her mother's house. Go through everything and get it ready to sell. She's planning to stay awhile, looks like. She asked about you, and I told her."

"Told her what?"

"Well, she just asked things *about* you. You know, about your life. Like what you'd done for a living, where you lived and if you had a family, and so forth. Things like that."

I've always thought Suzanne would know things about my life, but why did I think that?

"She didn't know I was back?"

"She didn't know *anything*. Asked me if you had any children. She talked to Charlotte more than she did to me. Charlotte said her husband died last year of a heart attack. He was around my age, I believe, maybe a little older. She has two grown children and a granddaughter. Lives up near Raleigh. Said she used to be a school teacher. Charlotte told her how sick you are, and she said she'd like to see you. She thought maybe you'd come to church. Charlotte told her you wouldn't."

"Yeah, I won't be doing that."

He tosses the empty can on top of the trash bag. "Suit yourself. I'm just telling you what she said."

*79.*

In November of my first year, the college lecture series brought in a well-known African-American poet who went by the single name of Aisha—her real name was Margaret Taylor—and in March the black power activist L. R. Sterling came to speak.

Camille was asked to introduce the poet. She described her body of work, praised the compelling music of her lines, her commitment to truth, and the startling depth of her vision. The reading lasted a little over half an hour.

Aisha thanked Camille, and she thanked the college for the invitation. Before she read her poems, she said it was important to place her work in the context of the times. She said it was incumbent on all black people to know the criminal history of the place they lived in.

"You think you already know it," she said, "but you really don't." She held up a sheaf of papers.

"What I'm holding in my hand here is a partial list of the lynchings and acts of terror that have taken place in this state, most of which you have never heard about. You know about some of these, of course, but there are *thousands* here," and she raised the sheaf and shook it.

"Thousands. And when you sit down to write your own poems—or to get ready to do *whatever* work you're going to do—these thousands of lost brothers and sisters—and not just lost but sadistically humiliated and tortured—these lives and souls should always be with you. They are counting on you to tell the truth.

"I'm going to read you a list of some of the Georgia towns and cities where lynchings have taken place. There are those of you here today—and there will be many of you, I promise—who will be surprised to hear me call the name of the town you grew up in, but you need to hear it.

"These atrocities took place in Columbus, Atlanta, Bainbridge, Colbert, Davisboro, Eastman, Valdosta, Statesboro, Watkinsville, Sparta, Montezumaa, Americus, Hazelhurst, Barnesville, Augusta, Macon, Leesburg, Talbotton, Athens, Cartersville, LaGrange, Monticello, Thomasville, Cuthbert, Cochran, Arabi, Tarrytown, Rome, Lincolnton, Newton, Marietta, Palmetto, Waycross, Griffin, Moreland, Donaldsonville, Cordele, Fort Valley, Lakewood, Darien, Elberton…." She read names for a while longer, then stopped and said she wasn't even a third of the way to the end.

I thought I heard her say Monroe. I did hear her say Monroe, but I had no idea what she was referring to.

"Let me tell you about just one of these crimes, a recent one that I think about every day, and about which I have written a poem."

She told the story of the 1964 murder of United States Army Lieutenant Colonel Lemuel Penn, "gunned down by the Klan while he was wearing the uniform of his country, shot down on the Broad River Bridge, up in Madison County, where the killers were acquitted by a white jury in an hour. Right here in this state where you live—this state that is still a battleground." Then she read the poem.

That evening, there was a reception at Claude and Arlene's house. I was not invited, but I didn't expect to be. It was mostly administrators and the English faculty. Walt and Lisa were there.

## *80.*

I was heading for my carrel and met Camille on the stairs.

“So, who is Mr. Charles?”

“What possessed you to ask me that?” She was not pleased.

“Isaac gave me some of your poems, and I saw there was a Mr. Charles in a couple of them, and I just wondered who that was.”

“Look, I don’t really want to talk about my poems, and he shouldn’t have let you see them. It was not his place to do that.”

“I thought they were good.”

“Oh, *did* you? And what made them good?”

“I can’t exactly say. I don’t know much about poetry. I don’t usually get it.”

“And so did you get *mine*?”

“I’m not sure, maybe not, but I guess I want to know who Mr. Charles is.”

“I’ll tell you what. You ask Wallace Lee about Mr. Charlie. He’ll be able to help you on that.” She continued down the stairs. “Sweet dreams.”

“Oh,” I said, “and I’ve been meaning to ask you. Did you ask Aisha to read any of your poems?”

She kept moving and didn’t look back. “I wouldn’t have done that in a thousand years.”

## *81.*

from *Bootleg Yesterday*

### LET MISTER CHARLES TRY TO EXPLAIN

He was not white

like picked cotton, not white

like bleached bone, not a white
that held the other colors, not

a wedding-veil white,
not a pearl-of-great-price white.

He was a mighty dirty white,
I know that. But guess what?

He's out there under the dirt,
and his skin is a bit too…what?

Oh, I know it's not fair. It's not.

*82.*

"Moon," Dr. Caruthers said, "today I heard your name used as a transitive verb."

She was on the Judiciary Committee, which had ruled on a case brought by female student accusing a male student of sticking his exposed buttocks out a dorm room window as she stood below.

"I couldn't help thinking of you."

I was beginning my third year at the college when she said this to me. I know exactly when it was because of a story in the news the following week, after which she appeared in the doorway of my office.

"Moon," she said, "I see your name is very close to being a verb again. Not quite there this time, but close. Your man Earl Butz, your Secretary of Agriculture—the man's name is Butz, you see—has metaphorically mooned every black person in America. Your man Butz has shown his ass, Moon."

I'd read the story in the newspaper and seen it on TV. Butz had been on a commercial flight to California after the 1976 Republican National Convention, along with Pat Boone, Sonny Bono, and John Dean, and he had been entertaining them. He told a joke that involved intercourse between a dog and a skunk. Pat Boone, a right-leaning Republican, tried to shift the conversation toward politics, and he asked Butz why the party of Lincoln was not able to attract more blacks.

Butz replied, "I'll tell you what the coloreds want. It's three things: first, a tight pussy; second, loose shoes; and third, a warm place to shit." The joke became public in October of 1976, and Earl Butz was forced to resign.

Dr. Caruthers said, "Moon, what is wrong with your people?"

I told her I didn't speak for my people, and they didn't speak for me.

"You might be right about that," she said, "and you might not, but listen, this is what I want to know: why are people calling that a *joke*? What makes it a joke? And if it *is* funny to somebody, why is it funny? Well, I suppose we do know the answer to that, don't we—I guess we do—but joke is not the word for what the man said. It's not a joke. It's something else."

*83.*

The day L. R. Sterling spoke in the gym, the crowd overflowed the stands and the playing floor and spilled out into the lobby. I stood on the court, behind the goal, leaning against the back wall. Mrs. Tolbert, a custodian in the Ayers building—quiet and relentlessly cheerful when she came in to take out my trash—stood next to me.

L. R. Sterling went straight to it.

"White people have lied to us and about us as long as this country has existed. They say 'All you have to do in this country is work hard, and you'll succeed.' They say, 'You people just don't want to work.'

"Work hard and you'll *succeed*? If that were the truth, we would own this whole country, lock, stock, and barrel. Ain't nobody ever worked harder than we have, the only people who literally slaved for this country. And got nothing for it.

"And now, now that we are supposed to *be* free, just let us actually *get* up in the world, *get* an education, *get* a nice house, *own* a place of business, what do they do? Look at what they did in Atlanta. Look at what they did in Tulsa.

"They said we got uppity, they said we got above our place, and they burnt us out. Went into our stores and our neighborhoods and burned them *down*. Brought rifles and pistols and took our lives, and then the newspapers called it a race riot and made it out like *we* had been the ones to riot.

"Our mothers scrubbed floors and ironed and cooked and cleaned for the white woman. Our fathers took off their hats and looked down and moved off the sidewalk for any white person—man, woman, or child. They did not suffer through those indignities so that we could do the same thing.

We in this generation must stand up and look the white man in the eye and say this is who we are. The moral weight of history is on *our* side, but white folks act like we need to please *them*."

Mrs. Tolbert said, "Preach, brother."

"Let's get it straight, people: The burden is not upon us to win the pleasure of those who have brutalized us and who continue to brutalize us. White America ought to be down on its knees every day of the week asking forgiveness for what it has done to black people and the innocent children of black people.

"Now, the white man is scared, he is outright terrified, that I will marry his daughter. Let's be clear: I have no *desire* to marry his daughter. But if I did, if I *did*, I would damn sure do what I wanted to do. And why not? The white woman is not the Virgin Mary. She's not the queen of the universe. She's a woman like any other woman.

"White people believe we want to sit next to them on the bus and in the restaurant and in the schoolroom. They act like we're just itching to slide in next to them and snuggle up, but we don't give a damn about sitting next to some white person. What's that supposed to do for us? What we want is the freedom to go where we *want* to go. We don't care if you're there or not. We just want you to get out of our way.

"The white man says we are culturally deprived. White folks must be blind. Everything we make, *everything* we come up with, they take it and act like *they* made it, and then say we are culturally deprived.

"Yes, we are indeed a deprived people. We are deprived of the very things we need just to keep on living, Mr. Charlie, if you want those things for yourself and you decide to take them.

"White folks call us uncivilized, they call us savages. Who is blowing up little girls in Sunday School? Whose dresser drawers hold souvenirs of lynchings? Bones and teeth polished up and put on a man's keychain or a little white girl's charm bracelet."

As L. R. Sterling came to the end, he changed it up and spoke directly to the students.

"You need to get to *work*," he said. "You need to be carrying around more in your heads than you are carrying around right now. Let me ask you this: Have you *read* Frederick Douglass, have you *read* Franz Fanon and W. E. B. Du Bois and Claude McKay and Leroi Jones?

"And why not? Maybe because all that Nadinola cream is messing with your head, you got your process going on, trying to ride up in that Fleetwood, ride up in that Bonneville, or imitating the white girls, trying to be the debutante, got the cotillion on your mind, throwing your little soror whoop across the yard, but only playing at a true sisterhood.

"None of that is *worthy* of you, not now, not in *this* day and age. This is the best chance you'll ever have to make your minds into *weapons*, people, and you need to go on and get to it."

## *84.*

The next day, Yusef Ishmael called me over. He tapped on the hardback ledger open in front of him. "I saw you down there yesterday. I recorded your presence." He believed we were living in revolutionary times, and that future generations would want to know the details of how everything had changed.

The ledger was open to a page holding two paragraphs and a drawing I couldn't make out.

"Listen, you heard what the man said about the white woman. Said if he wanted to have himself a white woman, that's what he would do. So tell me this: can a brother go ahead and get with the white woman? Can he do that?"

I said the brother would probably have to take that up with the white woman.

"That's what you say, but you don't mean it. A little reckless eyeballing and you'd be out there with the rest of them, dragging the black man into the piney woods.

"Tell me this: what makes you think you ain't white? Come here and walk around and act like you ain't white. I guess you don't understand that you don't get a *say* in it."

## *85.*

Camille and I were sitting with Dr. Reid in his office. She had brought a small bound volume from the library, with copies of articles from it.

"Wallace Lee asked me to bring these copies for you." She handed me two articles.

"And I wanted you to get a look at the journal itself," Dr. Reid said. "*De Bow's Review* was published in New Orleans from 1846 to 1867 by J. D. B. De Bow. It was a place for people to argue in favor of slavery."

Both articles were by Samuel Cartwright, a white medical doctor. One article was entitled "Drapetomania, or the Disease Causing Negroes to Run Away."

"To this man Cartwright," Dr. Reid said, "the slave's attempt to escape was evidence of some disorder of the mind or spirit. You see, like so many other people, he had no doubt that slavery was good for the black man. He thought the black man possessed the brain capacity of a white child, and so he could not govern himself. He could only be happy in the position God intended for him, that of slave and servant.

"So Cartwright came up with an imaginary mental illness he called drapetomania, from *drapeto*, the Greek for runaway slave, and *mania*, which he translated as crazy. Why would somebody run away from a slavery that was to his benefit? He'd have to be crazy. Yeah, this genius had it all figured out. He also said that the Bible, if translated properly, called the Negro 'the submissive knee-bender,' and he claimed that the Negro's knees were, in fact, anatomically suited for his divinely prescribed role, in that they were more flexed or bent than the knees of any other kind of man."

The other article was entitled "Unity of the Human Race Disproved by the Hebrew Bible." Dr. Reid said, "This man had a mighty high opinion of himself, I'll say that much. He didn't just solve all these Negro mysteries, he made himself out to be a biblical scholar and a theologian too. He goes ahead and sets everybody straight, once and for all, about what went on in the Garden of Eden."

*86.*

Jarvis was in a wreck. Walt and I drove to the hospital in Waycross. We were told that the man sitting alone in the waiting room outside the ICU was Jarvis's father.

He was bent over, elbows on his knees, his forehead resting on clasped hands as if he were praying, but his eyes were open. After a while, Walt asked him what the doctors said. He didn't look up.

"They say he's going to die."

I never heard him speak again.

The family buried Jarvis in a private ceremony at the family gravesite in Bainbridge. Dr. Plant was there, I understand, and so was Danielle, and I don't know who else.

Walt and I went over to Jarvis's house and fed his fish and stood looking at the box of light that had taken on the aura of a shrine. The black mollies and the black skirt tetras were as alive and as wide-eyed as ever, and Jarvis was in the past.

*87.*

It was late May, at the end of my first year at the college. Claude and I walked out of Regulus Hall at the same time, coming from an absurdly drawn out and unnecessary meeting.

"Only so many hours in a lifetime," he said, and he gestured behind him with the small book he held in his left hand, "and there went two of them."

We walked out into the cool of the evening, a heavy sweetness of magnolias in the air. A white 1960 Chevrolet Impala rolled past on College Street.

"I used to own that car," he said. "Look at those fins."

"My brother Donnie had one of those."
"Is that right? He liked it, didn't he?"
"He loved it."
"Yeah, that was a good car."

*88.*

The next day, Claude came to my office, something he had never done before. "I started to give you this yesterday," he said. "I want you to keep it. It's yours." He handed me his worn copy of *The Denial of Death* by Ernest Becker, with passages marked and notes in the margin.

"If you read it seriously, you'll find a lot to think about. And for a teacher of psychology, this might turn out to be an important perspective."

Notes from pages 68–69, with Claude's comments in brackets:

-in the myth of the Garden of Eden is found the basic insight of psychology for all time: man is a union of opposites, of self-consciousness and of the physical body [not sure those are opposites]

-man emerged from the instinctive thoughtless action of the lower animals and came to reflect on his condition, was given a consciousness of his individuality and his part-divinity in creation, the beauty and uniqueness of his face and his name; also given consciousness of the terror of the world and of his own death and decay

—this has been a constant in all periods of history and society

—the true "essence" of man: to be a creature, an animal, but with a symbolic inner identity, once called the soul [what can we call it now?]

—to have emerged from the ignorance of the beast, into the soulish i.e. the state of being conscious of the self and therefore, of death

—a creature, a beast capable of dread

—Kierkegaard: "Further than this psychology cannot go…and moreover it can verify this point again and again in its observation of human life."

*89.*

*And the serpent said unto the woman, Ye shall not surely die: For God doth know that in the day ye eat thereof, then your eyes shall be opened, and ye shall be as gods, knowing good and evil.*

*—Genesis 3:4,5*

It may have been a joke, but it was not a funny joke. Perhaps too subtle, coming as it did from the serpent, the most subtle, it is said—and by God himself—of all the creatures God made.

Was it a practical joke?

Surely the woman smiled. The apple was crisp and sweet in her mouth as her eyes were being opened to her own body and to the body of the man, and to the divine.

And what is the soul of irony, if not two truths at once?

No, you will not surely die, not right away, but you *will* surely die, and you will die like a god, able to understand what is happening and knowing also that you do not understand, that you can never understand, although you do.

# PART TWO

*We may be in the universe as dogs*
*and cats are in our libraries, seeing*
*the books and hearing the conversation,*
*but having no inkling of the meaning*
*of it at all.*

*—William James*

W*e, who are last year's dust and rain..*

*—Loren Eiseley*

*1.*

This story is true. I may have told it poorly so far—it's hard for me to know—but I have no special talent for telling a story. I know I have missed a lot and surely got things wrong. I have put myself at the center, but I don't know how else to do it. It's my life. I've tried to give clear descriptions, without providing much analysis, but since I don't really have much analysis to offer, that's not too difficult. When I've been confused, I hope I've owned up to it. I have made an effort to recall what others said and how they said it, and to avoid speculating on their motives or feelings. I've tried not to be presumptuous, but presumption is surely built into the telling of stories that include other real people. These days, I have a sense of unreality about what has taken place. The logic of time itself seems flawed, as though some irrational element has always been in control, able to move things around in time, even this late. When I look back now, I don't feel like I have awakened from a dream, but *into* one. And that's the truth, or my name is not Everett Moon.

*2.*

The consent decree was handed down late in the summer of 1974, so the college needed to hire a white person, although there was no time to carry out a proper search. Dr. Reid and the committee decided to find a placeholder, a marginally qualified person who would be easy to let go after the first year and who would not be likely to charge racial bias. They also intended that there be none. The position had to be tenure-track, but they viewed it as temporary, and they planned to hire a white person with a PhD after a regular search had been done. They were not trying to circumvent the consent decree, but to handle it in a way that was of maximum long-term benefit to the college, while also avoiding legal entanglement. Dr. Plant's friend Harris Luck was then the only black professor in the Psychology Department at the University of Georgia. Dr. Plant called him and told him what the search committee was looking for. I had taken Dr. Luck's History of Psychology class as an undergraduate, and he was aware that I was struggling with my graduate classes. He knew I would be fortunate to get a job. I knew none of this until many years after it happened.

*3.*

In 1985, the college was given more faculty positions, and the department hired two African-American women. I never got to know either of them well, although we were on good terms working together. At least I think we were. Neither has a voice in this story, which is one of the many ways in which it may be seen as narrow. It's mainly about my life and my first year at the college. When these professors were added to the department, ten years later, it became one of the strongest on campus. The year after they arrived, we added thirty-eight majors. Dr. Elena Jameson had a PhD. from Emory and did research on the use of biofeedback techniques in the treatment of high blood pressure. Her husband, an Army major, taught in the ROTC program. Dr. Maureen Allen held a doctorate from Howard. She taught Quantitative Methods and Experimental Psychology, but her main research interest was the psychology of African-

American humor. Our ongoing banter often involved both of us puzzling over how I got a psychology degree in the first place, given my poor grasp of quantitative methods. Until last spring, I continued to be offered a yearly contract as a senior instructor, and to teach introductory courses. What I have called a dismissal was technically not. My usual contract for a year was simply not offered.

*4.*

I'm reading a magazine at the library when Suzanne sits down beside me. The elevator pings and groans open, a woman steps out, holding a little girl by the hand. A man limps past our table, steadies himself on a chair and shuffles away, and the air has gone sour with sweat and a sickening musky tang. The homeless are often here. People must think I'm one of them, and in a way, I am.

We walk to the new sandwich place up the street, where the pool room used to be. She has a glass of wine. I have ginger ale. I let her know I've been sober for seven years.

The pool room used to smell like burnt grease and strong onions and oniony sweat, the air hazed over with cigarettes and cigars. It had three pinball machines, six pool tables, and a counter where you could sit and eat. I liked the pool room's hot dogs, but this was where I first heard there was an acceptable level of rat hair and insect parts in hot dogs, and that the meat did not exclude any part of the animal—rectum, eyeball, testicle, brain—all ground and pressed together with bits of rat droppings and cockroach wing. I didn't eat hot dogs for maybe a week after I heard that. Then I pushed it out of my mind, apparently for good. At times I think that's what I do best.

The restroom is where it always was, but once there was a urinal that overflowed, a blackened sink, a slick, sticky floor, a stench to sting your nose and eyes, profanities and racial slurs and bad cave drawings of genitals on the walls, though often the light bulb was busted or burned out and when the door closed you couldn't see a thing, and all you could do was step up and aim.

The restroom now is a clean cubicle of light and sanitizer and floral potpourri, with a fan and an automatic towel dispenser, an immaculate sink, and a mirror with an old man in it. There's clearly something wrong with him.

I'm not feeling well and I tell Suzanne I need to leave. We walk slowly back toward the library.

### *5.*

That day long ago when I went to Claude's office and we had our one long talk, the day he told me Arlene was going through something but I didn't ask him what—that same day, I asked Camille. She said Arlene had bone cancer. "She's very sick. She's been going through chemo again. Could you truly not tell?" I couldn't. I couldn't see what was right in front of me. Arlene had lost her hair and wore a wig. I didn't know that.

### *6.*

Jarvis had been spending time with the nurse for maybe three months. He never talked to me about her, but he talked to

Dr. Plant. Over the years, Dr. Plant told me parts of what he knew.

He said Jarvis and Nicole fought nearly every time they were together. They fought and made up and fought again. They would drink wine and they'd talk for hours, and they'd make love and sleep that good sleep, but the next day they'd take up their old troubles again. Nicole was a master of sabotage. She didn't trust happiness. Her life had taught her that to trust was always a mistake. If things were going really well for her, eventually she would feel happy, an unnatural feeling that needed to be killed. She would enjoy it as long as she could, and then she'd kill it, using one of the many maneuvers she had perfected.

Nicole was a virtuoso of emotional pain. For Jarvis, she was suffering and relief all at once—partly sexual healing, partly the wound itself. *Love* was a word Dr. Plant doubted in general—romantic love, that is—but Jarvis said he loved Nicole, and Dr. Plant took him at his word. That last day, they'd had a terrible argument. Jarvis got in his car to leave, Nicole got in too, and he was driving fast and they were shouting when Nicole tried to jump out of the car. Jarvis grabbed her wrist and jerked the steering wheel and the car rolled. Before she moved back to Atlanta, Dr. Plant asked Nicole if she had really meant to jump out of the car, and she told him she didn't know.

## 7.

Suzanne calls to see if I'm all right. We meet at Denny's, and we sit where I always do, in a booth by the window. I can see my room from here and I point it out. Juanita comes over and right away they discover they know some of the same people, having both grown up here.

When we're alone, I say what I meant to say the last time. I offer my condolences on the loss of her husband. She says it's been especially hard on his children.

She tells me about her son, Thomas, a writer and musician and the editor of a weekly newspaper in southern Virginia—he and his wife have a little girl—and about her daughter, Marie, who has just graduated from college and moved to Chicago to be an actor.

"They're both very talented," she says, looking me straight in the eye with an ease and a seriousness that says she's comfortable with the truth of what she's telling me. We talk about Charlotte and Donnie a little, and then about some of the people we used to know. She asks why I never got married.

"I did get married. I was married for less than a year to a former student, a woman the same age as me. I was thirty-two at the time. She got pregnant, and so we got married, and then we lost the baby, and that was it."

"Nobody told me."

"Almost nobody knows, I guess."

"I was surprised to find out you taught at a black college. What was that like?"

"Well, it was good. It was a good job to have."

"Did you have many friends?"

"I had some friends, yeah. Maybe not what you'd call really close friends, but I had a few."

"You said she was a former student, the woman you married. Was she black?"

"No, she was white. The white students trickled in. There weren't many."

"I guess what surprises me the most is that you ended up teaching. I never saw you as a teacher."

I can't help laughing, and I can tell she's relieved to be able to laugh too.

"I was surprised by it myself. It was an accident, really, the result of an odd sequence of events."

"I guess I'm interested in hearing how someone accidentally becomes a teacher."

Juanita brings our check. She tells Suzanne she has made the connection between her and an elderly couple who used to eat here.

"I just realized that was your mama and daddy. I can see the resemblance."

Suzanne insists on paying the check and steps to the counter. I sit here studying the space she no longer occupies, and I find myself remembering a day from 1965 when I was eating lunch in the school cafeteria. Suzanne was a few tables over, sitting with three other girls, when one of the black girls—one of the four who had desegregated the school that year—took a seat at the far end of the long table. The other white girls picked up their trays and moved, but Suzanne kept her seat. She didn't intend to make a big statement, she told me later. She just didn't feel like being inconvenienced. That afternoon, she opened one of her books to find obscenities written all through it.

## *8.*

Carol Watts took my introductory class, an elective for her major in business. She was my age and the only white student in a class of forty. She needed the credits to graduate that summer and chose my section because she'd heard it was easy.

In the fall she took a job as a teller in a local bank. We spoke when I went there to deposit my check, and I started to find reasons to return, which amused her.

We went out for a while, she got pregnant, and we agreed to get married. Neither of us had seen that anywhere in our future with one another. At six months, they told us the baby had no heartbeat. She underwent a delivery, and the horror—that's the word she used—of what she endured freed her to tell me the truth.

I was not somebody she could continue to be around, she said. There was a strange distance about me that made her uneasy. And I needed to stop drinking.

*9.*

Walt asked Dr. Caruthers to explain Zora Neale Hurston's opposition to the Brown decision.

"It's not exactly what it seems," she said. "You see, she felt *insulted* by the decision. She did write a letter to a newspaper that southern politicians were very pleased to use for their own purposes, but you have to understand the context. As a child, she had gone to an all-black school, a good school, in an all-black town. She knew that the presence of white students and teachers in a school was not required for black students to receive a quality education. Provide equal resources, and there would be no need for integration. Of course, she knew resources would not be made equal, she knew Jim Crow was a criminal regime that had to end, and she knew integration was a necessity. But she still thought it wrong that black children should be subjected to sitting next to white children who from birth had been taught the myth that they were superior."

*10.*

William James once found himself dreaming two dreams at the same time, and the next night, he dreamed three. That first night, a peaceful dream was suddenly joined with something violent and tragic, involving wild animals. The next night, there was a dream set in London, interwoven with two dreams set in America—one having to do with a coat, and one that was a nightmare having to do with soldiers....

"I began to feel curiously confused and scared," he said, "and tried to wake myself up wider, but I seemed already wide-awake.... Presently a cold shiver of dread ran over me: am I getting into other people's dreams? Is this a 'telepathic' experience? Or an invasion of double (or treble) personality? Or is it a thrombus in a cortical artery? and the beginning of a general mental 'confusion' and disorientation which is going on to develop who knows how far?"

James called it "a state of consciousness unique and unparalleled in my 64 years of the world's experience."

*11.*

The waitress says, "Hey there, sweetie, what's the occasion?" I don't know what she's asking me. She waves her pencil at my clothes, and I see that I'm dressed for my own funeral, in a black suit, with a white shirt and a tie. I'm wearing my old black dress shoes, and someone has polished them. "Oh, hon, are you all right?" She calls Juanita, who comes over and slides into the booth with me. She says, "Hey, Everett. Don't worry, now. It'll be all right. Don't cry, now. Everything's going to be all right." They call Donnie. He sits across from me and raps on my hand with his knuckles. He says, "What's going on, little brother?" and he takes me to the emergency room.

They keep telling me I've had a transient ischemic attack. Maybe I keep asking. There's something new and unwieldy inside that fishtails all through me, back and forth between crying and laughing. Off and on all day, I've had lucid dreams where I'm awake inside the dream and able to control what I do. I get out of bed and walk down the hospital hallway. I visit the boy two doors down who had a seizure and fell and broke his left wrist. He's a left-handed pitcher and he's scared now, he's questioning who he is, if he's not a baseball player. I want to help him, but I can't. I'm dreaming.

*12.*

A white man I don't know comes in and introduces himself as Reverend someone from somewhere. He pulls a chair close to the bed and holds up one of those small green Gideons, about the size of a pack of playing cards.

"I'm going to leave this with you," he says, "if that's all right." He lays it on the bedside table.

I say sure. I guess he thinks I don't own a bible.

"Would you mind if we said a word of prayer?" He goes ahead. "Heavenly Father…"

I feel myself right at the edge of saying, "For once, can't you just shut your damn mouth?" But I stop it and ask him if we can maybe hold off a minute.

"Absolutely," he says, "If that's the way you want it. But let me just go on and ask you this, my friend: Do you know where you'll be spending eternity?"

I feel a lurch toward sorrow but then I'm laughing, and I realize the question was not funny until the laughter overtook me. And I know if I started to cry, the question would turn sad, and somehow would have *always* been sad.

Reverend someone gets to his feet and appears to consider picking up the little Gideon. I go ahead and ask him to forgive me. I tell him I didn't mean to be disrespectful. I say I don't know where I'll be spending eternity, but I don't think I'll be spending it anywhere, and that's what I hope for too.

## *13.*

Out some window—I'm not sure where—the clouds are torn into oddly angled shreds. Suzanne would know what to call them.

I keep on losing the word *ischemic*, a word I've known all my adult life. I try to call it up as I remind myself what has happened to me, but it doesn't come back, it's not automatic anymore, and I have to ask.

I've been with Donnie and Charlotte for three days. They insist it's time for me to move in with them for good. I'm not doing that. We're all in the TV room. Iris has been watching a cartoon, but now she's playing on the floor with her animals, talking for them.

Charlotte raises her voice. "You are *not* moving back to that motel." Iris looks up quickly. "We're not going to let you *do* that. It's not safe for you to be there by yourself. You're going to stay right here."

I told her I was not. "I'm going to make my own decisions for as long as I can. One of you needs to drive me back over there."

"*Look*," Donnie says, "you didn't even know where the hell you *were* the other day. There's no *telling* what could have happened. What if you'd started out driving? You could have hurt somebody. You need to stay at least another day or two. We've got the room all fixed up now, we've already got lots of your things in there. What's in that stinking motel room that's better than what you got here?"

"I need to go on back, and that's what I plan to do. I might call a taxi."

Iris has an elephant in one hand and a horse in the other. She's leaning against the sofa cushion between Charlotte and me. She speaks for the elephant: "I'm the biggest," and she gives me the horse and says, "*Talk* him," and I find myself talking him.

## *14.*

Sick in bed all morning. Can't get my lungs full. Can't get comfortable in any position. A burning pain at the base of my skull. My ears ache. The back of my tongue is raw. A metallic, bitter taste. Thick coughing all night in the motel room next to mine. A racket of carts in the hallway. I get out of bed and take a few sips of Sprite and eat a saltine and try not to throw up, then go ahead and try to throw up, but can't.

In bed again, there's poison in the dream air, a buzzing low overhead in the dream sky; a crop duster unloads a cloud into my face. I wake up struggling for breath. Who was flying that plane? I realize I was hearing the vacuum cleaner in the hall and smelling disinfectant, but I still want to find out who thought it was necessary to fly so low over where I was trying to sleep.

*15.*

Yesterday when I got ready to take a shower, I took off all my clothes, then put on a T-shirt and started to get in the shower but something stopped me. I stepped back and stood there, unable to see exactly what was wrong until I gave up and got in and turned on the water and that's when I figured it out. Last night, reading a newspaper, I pulled a tissue from a Kleenex box, put it in my lap, then blew my nose on the newspaper.

Suzanne calls to ask how I'm doing. I don't tell her any of this. I tell her about the young woman who filled my prescription at Carmichael's this morning, who wanted me to remember that "all things work together for good to those who love God." I know she meant well, but I have never found love of any kind to be an act of will.

*16.*

There's a video I showed often in class, about a British classical musician named Clive Wearing who contracted a virus that destroyed his hippocampus and temporal lobes bilaterally, so that none of his short-term memories could ever be transferred to long-term.

Clive was trapped in the present and the distant past, becoming ever more distant. You could tell him the same joke or the same bad news repeatedly—he would always forget it. He lost everything but the far past, and he could never understand what had happened to him. Over and over, he felt he had just awakened, for the first time in a long time. He asked, "Can you imagine a night two years long?"

But he recognized Deborah, his wife, whom he loved deeply, and every time she came into the room, he leapt to his feet and embraced her as if he hadn't see her in years, though she might have left the room only minutes before. He would swing her in his arms and sing. In line after line of his diary he wrote, "Awake for the first time now, and I adore Deborah forever."

*17.*

After a summer trip to Ivory Coast, a student named Montez Reese said to me, "Man, I'm glad y'all put us on the boat."

I didn't know what to say to that.

"You had a rough time?"

"You wouldn't believe it. I couldn't live like that. I'm glad y'all put us on the boat."

So he'd said it again.

"Really? You're glad people were slaves because now you have such a good life here?"

"That's not what I'm saying. Don't put words in my mouth. I'm saying I'm glad I don't have to live like that. Don't *ever* put words in my mouth."

A few times—more than a few, I admit—I entered the classroom trying to pull off a pimp roll. I walked with a slight limp anyhow because of my bad knee. So I dipped a shoulder, threw in a little hesitation, and slid on in, intending this as an ironic act—at least that's how I remember it—and wishing to be seen as intentionally ridiculous. I hoped I would be seen as the butt of my own joke, that no one would see it as an act of mockery. I counted on being seen as a clown and a fool, and I was pretty well successful at that, I still believe, though maybe not as often as I thought, and maybe even if I *was* the butt of my own joke, it was rude and offensive anyway. Maybe it was. I'm sure it was. But if that's true, how do I talk about it now? Maybe I don't. Maybe I ought to be quiet.

## *18.*

Not long before he died, Dr. Reid showed me some pages from the beginning of his book about lynchings in the state of Georgia, which he'd been working on for so many years.

The passage was about the 1946 lynchings at Moore's Ford, not far outside Monroe. It included two newspaper stories.

*New York Times* July 27, 1946

**Georgia Mob Massacres**

**Two Negroes and Wives**

Monroe, Ga., July 26—Two young Negroes, one a veteran just returned from the war, and their wives were lined up last night near a secluded road and shot dead by an unmasked band of twenty white men. Names of the victims have not yet been released.

Details of the multiple lynching were told by Loy Harrison, a well-to-do white farmer who had just hired the Negroes to work on his farm. Harrison was bringing the Negroes to his farm when his car was waylaid by the mob eight miles from Monroe. Harrison said that one of the Negroes was suspected of having stabbed his former employer, a white man.

The two men were removed from the car and led down a side road, and when the women began to scream, they were dragged from the car and taken down the same road.

A few moments later, Mr. Harrison heard shots, many of them, and then the mob dispersed. The grotesquely sprawled bodies were found in a clump of bushes, the upper parts of the bodies scarcely recognizable from the mass of bullet holes.

The mother of one of the victims said that her son had just been discharged after five years in the Army and that she had received his discharge button in the mail just this week.

*New York Times* July 29, 1946

**Relatives Shun Funeral of Negroes**

**Lynched in Georgia**

Monroe, Ga., July 28—Close relatives of two of the four Negroes killed by a white mob here last week failed to appear at funeral services today. Friends voiced the opinion that they were too frightened to appear.

Dr. Reid said, "It wasn't until your job interview that I found out where you were from. I'd been doing research on Moore's Ford, and then here *you* show up. So I wanted to talk with you a little during that academic year and then let you go your own way. That was always the plan, but of course, you knew nothing about it. It was up to me to initiate a search to replace you, but I never did. After what happened with our friends, I was pretty well paralyzed right along then, I'll admit. I saw what it did to you too. Then I looked a little more closely at your background, and I began to feel some responsibility for having brought you here under false pretenses. I didn't want to feel like that, but that's how I felt. In allowing you to continue here, I did not serve our students well. I know that now. And I knew it then. But what's done is done."

I said, "But you never asked me about Moore's Ford."

"Not directly I didn't, no."

## *19.*

I knew nothing about the lynching until three years after the college hired me. I heard about it as I was driving my grandmother to Emory Hospital the day of her surgery, the day she died.

She asked me if I knew anything about four colored people being killed by a mob outside of Monroe back in 1946. It had made headlines in New York, she said, and President Truman got involved with the case.

How was it possible that such a thing happened in the small town where I grew up, and I knew nothing about it?

## *20.*

Dr. Plant and his twin brother grew up on a dairy farm near Augusta. Their parents worked for the white family who owned the farm. He and his brother were up early every morning to help out with the milking before they went to school, then back home every afternoon to help out again. Dr. Plant always said there was nothing like working on a dairy farm to give you a desire for an education. The work was seven days a week, month after month, year after year.

When he graduated from high school, Dr. Plant enrolled at Paine College, got a graduate degree from Florida A&M, and started teaching. Then he went to Ohio State for his doctorate. He did this under a state-sponsored fellowship program that supported black faculty at Georgia colleges who pursued graduate studies out of state, a program designed to discourage qualified black instructors from applying to state universities.

His brother didn't attend college, but he had done well for himself. He learned plumbing while in the Army, and after being discharged, he moved to Atlanta, where he was eventually able to set up his own shop. He made a good living.

Though it was an impossible task, given the explosion of data, Dr. Plant tried to stay current with the literature in several fields of psychology. He saw himself as a generalist, which was the best approach to take, he said, if you're teaching undergraduates.

He had based his dissertation on the early research into cognitive errors, examining how those errors might have manifested themselves in rural black populations. He had published two papers in that area, but now he had stopped doing research, although he had recently developed an interest in what was being called cultural mistrust, defined as a tendency of minority populations to be mistrustful of those in the majority. Some researchers had used the term cultural paranoia, but he believed such a term unnecessarily categorized as pathological what he saw as a real and powerful phenomenon involving both rational and irrational elements.

## *21.*

When we came to the topic of psychoanalysis in the intro course, I went to Dr. Plant to ask some questions, since I knew he had studied it quite a bit. He gave me several books, including a volume of Jung's essays, which he opened to a section he had marked.

"While you're reading about the basics, you might also take a look at this, since it affords an interesting perspective on Jung's ideas about race. It's from this essay called 'The Complications of American Psychology.' The part I'm talking about starts right here, where Jung is back in Switzerland after being in the United States. Let me read you this short passage. Jung says, 'When I returned from America, I was left with the peculiarly dissatisfied feeling of one who has somehow missed the point.... I had to confess that I was unable to size them up.

"I was once the guest of a pretty stiff and solemn New England family of a rather terrifying respectability.... There were Negro servants waiting at table. I felt at first as if I were eating lunch in a circus and I found myself diffidently scrutinizing the dishes, looking for the imprint of those black fingers.'"

Dr. Plant said, "Now here's the great psychoanalyst, a man renowned for his spiritual depth, and he feels like he's in a circus because black people are serving his food, and he finds himself studying the dishes to see if the black fingers have left an imprint. What exactly was he looking for, do you suppose? I suspect he was concerned about contamination from the touch of the black man. At least, that's how I see it. I'm sure there's another interpretation. Decide for yourself."

He read more: "A solemnity brooded over the meal for which I could see no reason, but I supposed it was the solemnity or serenity of great virtue or something like that which vibrated through the room. At all events nobody laughed. Everyone was just too nice and too polite. Eventually I could stand it no longer, and I began to crack jokes for better or worse. These were greeted with condescending smiles.... I came to my last story, really a good one, and no sooner had I finished than right behind my chair an enormous avalanche of laughter broke loose.

"It was the Negro servant, and it was the real American laughter, that grand, unrestrained, unsophisticated laughter revealing rows of teeth, tongue, palate, everything, just a trifle exaggerated.... How I loved that African brother.' "

Dr. Plant said, "Now, Jung may have read the situation correctly. It's very likely that he did, by which I mean that the black man found the joke to be funny. But it's also possible that the servant had already heard a succession of unfunny jokes and had witnessed the lack of response at the table, and that when the final joke bombed too, he could not hold back his laughter, he just couldn't.

"That's entirely possible. I'm sure he would have *intended* his response to be taken just as Jung took it, since laughing at the great man's lame performance would have been disrespectful, and it's not likely the servant would have taken such a risk, but the joke itself provided his cover. It's also true, though—and this is why I'm pointing it out—that the laughter of black people has often been *profoundly* misread."

## *22.*

A student wanted to know if it was true that when a person falls to his death, his whole life passes before his eyes. I asked him how we could possibly know that, since the dead can't testify. The dead can indeed testify, two members of the class let me know, and a discussion of the afterlife and other supernatural matters followed.

I told them William James agreed with their position, or was open to it at least. In his final days, he had asked his brother Henry to stay in Cambridge for six weeks after the funeral. William would try to contact him from beyond the grave. Apparently, that did not happen.

But the question of reviewing one's life while falling was also a chance for students to consider the problem of human limitation, a topic relevant to psychology in a variety of important ways.

People once believed human thought to be the fastest entity in the universe. Estimates of the speed of the nerve impulse had been as high as sixty times the speed of light, or 11.16 million miles per second.

But in 1849 Hermann von Helmholtz found a way to measure it and discovered the true velocity was close to 120 meters per second—somewhere around 270 miles per hour, not forty billion. In a second, it travels maybe a football field and a third instead of 448 orbits of the planet. That's some mistake.

*23.*

Claude would ask his philosophy students to consider a housefly that touches down on a page of calculus:

"The fly senses and interprets. It makes an inquiry, it searches for certain molecules, it picks up clues from the paper, it makes its discoveries. There are things it knows. But the equations and the graphs on the page, *as* equations and graphs, are beyond the housefly in an absolute way. We humans have our limits too, and we are subject to a beyond just as absolute. What is truly beyond us will *be* beyond us. It won't be explained in Genesis or accounted for by quantum theory or by anything else that can come alive in the human nervous system or its instruments. Not to acknowledge that, it seems to me, is vanity and foolishness."

*24.*

Elizabeth's husband is in jail on a charge of domestic violence. The neighbors complained, and when the police showed up, they found marks and bruises on Elizabeth's face and neck. One side of her mouth was swollen. She didn't want to file charges but the police took him to jail anyway.

When Donnie learned about this, he took his pistol from the safe in his bedroom and put it in his car.

## *25.*

Suzanne's friend Michelle died two days ago. Nobody called her till this morning, which she cannot believe. The funeral is at 11:00 today in Raleigh. When we talk on the phone, she can barely speak. "So I can't meet you," she says. "I've got some calls I need to make, and then I plan to work on the house for a while."

I say I'm sorry about her friend.

"I appreciate it, Everett, but listen, I can't get news like this and try to deal with it and look at *you* at the same time, I just can't. You need to know that."

I drive out Highway 11 toward Winder, stop in Campton and come back. I turn right on Spring Street and start feeling dizzy and pull over in front of a building that once housed Stowe's Lunchroom, across from the old Recreation Center.

Donnie and I used to play pinball at Stowe's, though our grandmother had forbidden it. She considered pinball a game of chance, and she was against anything associated with gambling. There were no playing cards in the house, and not even a Monopoly game, since dice were thrown.

I always thought she opposed games of chance because people could cause hardship for their families when they gambled and lost their money.

But one day she explained to me that since the will of God was revealed in everything—every leaf that fell, every dust mote swirling in the air—a roll of the dice was not based on chance. Instead, it showed the will of God and was an act of sacrilege, a revealing of the sacred in a tawdry and trivial fashion, a tempting of God and an unworthy glance at the divine plan.

### *26.*

Suzanne comes over. We sit on a sofa in the lobby. The light above us buzzes and flickers. I can't take that for long.

She says, "It's not like you and I have anything to straighten out between us. But I can tell you this, Everett. Whatever you may have imagined us going through over the years, it was worse than that. Whatever you might have imagined, it was many times worse than that. Because you can't imagine it."

And it hits me that I didn't imagine anything at all. I almost never thought about them. I must have a numb space inside where I've been keeping them.

"Don't you have any questions for me? Aren't you curious at all about the last thirty-six years? Did you ever *ask* anybody about us—Mama and Daddy and me? You didn't ask Donnie or Charlotte, from what they say. Did you ever try to contact us? You never called. Back then, if you had called me, I'm pretty sure I would have told you where to go and hung up—I *know* I would have—but at least you would have *tried.* You didn't reach out at all."

"But I did. I wrote you a letter, and I wrote them one, and nobody wrote me back. I took that to mean I should leave you alone."

"I didn't get a letter, and if Mama and Daddy got a letter, they said nothing about it. *When* did you write me a letter?"

"I wrote it at the beginning of the first quarter we were in college, and I wrote them one too."

"That's fine, Everett. Maybe you did. But we got no letters that I'm aware of."

"I did send them." I did.

"What did they say?"

"I can't remember now. I said I was sick to death. I said I wished it had been me instead of Leon."

"That's the sort of thing people say, isn't it?"

"I guess it is."

"When Mama went into Junior's room, it was like a blast knocked her back. Daddy tried to hold her, but she fought him off. She got down on her knees and beat her head against the hardwood floor. Daddy got down there and wrapped her up in his arms and stopped her and he held her for a long time like that, with her fighting to get away. They wouldn't go to bed that night. I made them go in the bedroom and I went with them, and we lay down on top of the covers and held one another and looked into the dark and sobbed and moaned and screamed. And that was just the beginning. From then on, we went through something that is really indescribable to somebody who has not gone through it. People use the word *nightmare*, but that's not the word. You wake up from a nightmare. But you never wake up from this, not really. You're going to have to leave me alone now."

## *27.*

I am living an imaginary life. If I had been seriously injured in the wreck, if I had been paralyzed or maimed or blinded, or suffered some other brutal injury, I'm sure that at times I would have imagined my life if I had walked away unhurt, as I did. I walked away unhurt. And that's the life I have now, in this world of grace and freedom that I can't really see for what it is.

*28.*

Dr. Reid had given me two articles by Samuel Cartwright from *De Bow's Review*. The first described drapetomania, the mental illness Cartwright invented to explain why slaves ran away. The second was entitled "Unity of the Human Race Disproved by the Hebrew Bible."

A quote from that article: "Nachash.... That is the name of the creature that beguiled Eve—the charmed—the enchanted—watching closely—prying into designs—muttering and babbling without meaning—hissing—whistling—deceitful—artful—fetters—chains—and a verb formed from the name, which signifies to be or to become black. Any good overseer would recognize the negro's peculiarities in the definition of Nachash."

"For white Christians, of course," Dr. Reid said, "there was always a need to justify the treatment of black people. Some held with a separate creation, saying the black man had been created with the animals, and some cited the curse of Ham. But this white man went even further and declared that the serpent of Genesis was 'the negro gardener.' It was the *Negro* who beguiled Eve. You see, the serpent of Genesis was the black man out there working in the garden. Wouldn't you know it?"

"Poor Eve," Camille said. "The white woman just can't catch a break, can she? Barely created, and there she is, already being sweet-talked by a brother."

*29.*

Late one night after a long day of meetings at a faculty retreat at a state park, Dr. Caruthers and I were having a drink, leaning back in low Adirondack chairs on a terrace overlooking the 18th green.

She told me she'd been struggling a little recently. The driver of the car that hit her son had died a few weeks ago, and his death had affected her in ways she didn't expect.

"He was twenty-five years old when it happened. A car mechanic. Married, with a four-year-old girl. A white man. I detested him for being alive while Odell was dead—and the girl too, not something I'm proud of—but I can see now that he was guilty of nothing but driving down the street.

"And I saw it at the time, too, I did. I couldn't accept it, though, not back then. I just couldn't. But the accident happened to him too, and as the years passed, I was reconciled to that. I'm not sure why his death has hit me so hard."

She told me about her conversation with Camille, who had just returned from Miami after staying with her sister, Angelina, during the last month of her life.

"They were very close, you know, and very much alike. I talked to Camille last week, just before her sister died, and then I talked to her again yesterday after she got back."

I had been at the college for twenty-one years. Dr. Caruthers had been retired for a while and was only visiting at the retreat, but she had gone to all the meetings. I told her she'd shown her true colors. She agreed and had a good laugh at herself.

I don't know what came over me then. I heard myself telling her I'd had a wreck in which a boy was killed.

She told me very softly that she knew. I didn't see how that could be. I'd never talked about it to anybody.

"One thing I *have* learned is this," she said. "What you think is a secret might not be a secret at all, and what you think is widely known, that just might be where your secret is. And listen, it's of absolutely no consequence how I came to know it. Trust me."

A wild shout reached us from the clubhouse, where they were playing cards, and we heard a voice we recognized that made us smile, and as it continued, made us laugh.

## *30.*

Camille had given a party at her house, and everybody else had left, but I'd drunk too much and was in no shape to drive yet. I was only weeks away from the end of my drinking life, but I didn't know it.

"Look," I said, "I can go out and sit in the car and close my eyes for a few minutes, and then I'll be okay."

"You stay right where you are." She told me just to go ahead and make myself comfortable.

This was the Saturday after the O. J. verdict.

"I was watching you earlier," she said, "you know, when Twin did his Johnnie Cochran voice. You had this look on your face."

I told her the whole thing had sort of thrown me off balance. I wasn't sure why. I was a little surprised by how big the reactions had been, both black and white.

"It's like I told you," she said. "This was not about O. J., not really, not to me anyhow. I'm only speaking for myself, you understand. Not everybody feels the way I do. But to me, this was about America turned upside down, with wealth and celebrity and influence on the side of the black man for once, so that this time it was a black man who was not held accountable for what he had clearly done, a result that has left some people feeling violated. I've heard it's a bad feeling."

Dr. Plant had imitated Johnnie Cochran talking about all the *righteousness* suddenly in the air, about people suddenly becoming so *righteous* about the *law*, saying how can this *happen*?

"Listen, I saw it on the news," Dr. Plant said. "White folks fixing to burn down their own gazebos."

"I know I'm burning *mine* down," I told Camille when she repeated what he'd said.

"You put a gazebo out back of your trailer?"

"And I'm burning it down. But come on, you know I don't live in that trailer anymore."

"Well, look, this is a good time to ask you: Why *did* you live in that trailer all those years? What was it, like fifteen years?"

"About that long, yeah, but I finally got an apartment."

I had lived in a rental house briefly while I was married, but when that ended, I moved back to the trailer park and lived there until they closed it. Camille knew that.

She put on a CD and came back to the sofa. "This is Sade's 'Love Deluxe,'" she said. "It was Angelina's, one of her favorites." I owned the same CD. I loved Sade's voice and still do. There's a kind of precise coolness in it.

We listened for a while. I told her I really didn't know why I'd kept on living in the trailer. "I tend to stay with what I know, I guess."

"Living there a long time is one thing," she said, "but living in a nice house and then going back there, well, that's something else."

"Yeah," I said, "I guess it is."

*31.*

**Angelina**

*for my sister in her illness*

The years are not a tragedy,
my Angelina, and they are not a joke either.

The evening is not what it was, yet tonight
in my dream we are out in the back yard,

the pear tree has blossomed out of season,
the winter grass is green, we are children

chasing one another. There is no one dream
or story that can hold our lives together.

We're full of all our days, we're full of all
those old, slow hours of the afternoon.

Do you hear the owl calling you? I don't,
little sister, or the train whistle either.

*32.*

The Board of Regents appointed Dr. Franklin Calder as president in the fall of 2000. He'd been a dean at Hampton and before that, a professor of economics there. A tall, thin, always impeccably dressed man in his late fifties, Dr. Calder was a moving orator and a brilliant politician. He sponsored a three-day conference last spring entitled "The HBCU: Where We Are Now," for which he brought in professors from historically black colleges and universities around the country.

There were lectures and panel discussions, and parts of the conference were televised on C-Span. Dr. Calder asked me to give a short talk, as one of the longest-serving white instructors. This surprised me and made me uneasy. I tried to decline, but he insisted. I worked on the talk for months, and it turned into a kind of autobiographical sketch, a series of short vignettes from my life that seemed relevant to my work at the college, although I didn't start out to write it like that.

I came across a few pages this morning. I thought I had destroyed all evidence of it.

**One Man's Perspective**
by Everett Moon

I want to thank President Calder for including me in this conference. I am truly humbled in this company. I want to begin by acknowledging that I cannot lend any broad perspective to the question of the current status of historically black colleges and universities. My experience is limited, and I have not studied the history of these institutions in any depth. All I can do, I'm afraid, is to tell a few stories about who I am and where I came from, and how I believe my history has influenced my time here.

A.

Mine was the last generation of southern white people to grow up in the old segregation. I could detail some aspects of that time in America, but I am standing before people who know infinitely more about it than I do, and who know it in a way that is qualitatively different from anything I can ever know.

I came straight here from the University of Georgia, still largely segregated at the time, and I have been here for 28 years. My experience has been an unusual one. I came into a microcosm of black control, of inverted power in a very specific and constricted way, where I worked *for* black people. And that has made a difference in my life.

I was a poor teacher at first, and I really deserved to be let go, but it was the late Dr. W. L. B. Reid who had brought me here, and for reasons of his own, he looked out for me. He did make it clear that I had to do better, but he allowed me to go on living and working in this community, which was an act of mercy. He's been gone almost ten years now, and I'm saddened by the knowledge that I fell short of justifying his faith in me. He deserved to know the whole truth.

B.

Dr. Reid corrected me when I needed correcting. He educated me about certain things he believed I needed to know. He gave me books to read. I didn't always read them. He would call me into his office to talk. He'd point out a few paragraphs and have me read them to myself while I sat there, and then he might ask me a question or have me ask him one. I read his book on Reconstruction, and we talked about it. We talked about his first book, *Patriotic Hypocrisy*, on lynchings and the black veteran. What he primarily wanted, I believe now, was to make sure that I had at least been exposed to this material.

Dr. Reid called it remedial education. He said, "Most people in this country *need* remedial education about its racial history, not just in the broad strokes but in the details that *make* it real, that make it come alive enough for people to feel it. Folks always ask, 'Why rehash all this? Well, it needs to be rehashed, because it was never hashed out in the first place, never seen clearly enough, never understood for what it was, never given the weight in human lives it deserved. People are ignorant of it, but they pretend they are not." Dr. Reid liked to say, "People are always pretending to have read the book when they haven't."

C.

I was sitting alone in Founders' Auditorium, at a Parents' Day program on a Saturday morning, looking down from the balcony at students giving flowers to their parents. I had been at this college for nineteen years. What came over me that day was not an idea or an insight. I had discovered nothing, I'd achieved no moral awakening. What I believe now is that my body understood something on its own, and I was hit with a wave of sorrow. I made it into the hall and headed for the door, about to sob and throw up at the same time.

D.

"Even if people do know history," Dr. Reid used to say, "that doesn't mean they know what to do with it."

Our talk about *Patriotic Hypocrisy* was coming to an end when he asked me if I had read his footnote on Thomas Jefferson. I've never been in the habit of reading footnotes, and I had not read that one.

"People always want to talk about Jefferson owning slaves," he said. He said you could expect a lot of talk about how the founding father responsible for writing 'all men are created equal' owned slaves—600 slaves over his lifetime. And you could expect people to talk about Sally Hemings too. But people don't talk as much about his "Notes on the State of Virginia," he said, which is where Jefferson makes straightforward white supremacist declarations.

The footnote includes this quote from Jefferson, about black people: "Their griefs are transient." The footnote is an addendum to Dr. Reid's discussion of the widespread sentiment throughout American history, and right up to today, that the loss of a black life is not equal to the loss of a white life.

"But there's this, too," Dr. Reid said to me that day. "What I'm about to tell you now is not part of my footnote because it lacks relevance, but you'll find this as well in "Notes on the State of Virginia." Jefferson writes that blacks themselves provide evidence for the superiority of whites by how 'the black race displays its preference for the white, as uniformly as is the preference of the Oranootan for the black women over those of his own species.'"

Dr. Reid wanted me to notice how casually Jefferson threw in what he took to be a given—that black women had mated with apes.

"Look," he said to me, "I *fought* for my country. I put my life on the line for the United States of America, and I was proud to do it. It was the right thing to do. But I do not hold with the deification of the founding fathers. When they wrote the Declaration of Independence and the Constitution, they were not writing holy scripture. And when Thomas Jefferson, great man that he sometimes was, wrote about race, when he wrote about the black woman mating with the ape, and when he diminished the lifelong suffering of black mothers who'd had their babies ripped from their arms—calling their grief *transient*—he was not great, and he was not good. He was ignorant and he was evil, and that needs to be said too."

E.

After all my time at this college, this is what I believe: There was real value in the mundane, in doing ordinary things together for a long time, year after year, common things common to us. There was real value in our days of tedious work; value in the slow lines we shared, in the routines, the forms, report after report, plan after plan, the milestones and the deadlines. There was real value in meeting after meeting, all the hours on committees, all the hours in assemblies, in years of being oriented regarding this or that, briefed on, made aware of, apprised of, instructed as to how and when, with regard to whatever it was. And there was a nearly transcendent value in workdays spent not looking *at* each other, but looking in the same direction, intent on what we thought we were headed toward, part of the same lumbering, awkward beast of an institution, completing small tasks in hopes of building something larger but never exactly knowing if we had done so, moving slowly toward some worthy tomorrow. It was a good thing to be doing ordinary and necessary work side by side, looking forward. I'm sure of it.

F.

But here is a part of my history I never told Dr. Reid, though I owed him the truth. One night in August, the summer before my senior year of high school, there was nothing to do in my hometown of Monroe, Georgia, but to ride up and down Highway 78, from the Tastee Freeze to the Dairy Queen and the Snack Shack and back. My girlfriend was in Daytona Beach with her parents and her brother. At the Dairy Queen my friends and I heard somebody say there was a Klan rally going on in a cow pasture a few miles out Highway 138. We had always heard about the Klan, but none of us had ever seen them. They were a relic of the past, about to become extinct, we believed. To us, they were a big joke, and we thought they would put on a good show. We could ride out there and kill the boredom.

There were maybe thirty people gathered on a slope just beyond the gate to the pasture. Ever since that evening, I've told myself I wasn't really in attendance at the meeting, since we didn't pass through the gate, didn't even get close to the fence but stood on the opposite side of the road. We were observers, I've always told myself. Spectators, that's all. We were not a part of what was going on. I realize now it doesn't work that way.

I hadn't thought it would be so familiar. A church service. Prayers, a sermon with a threatening, accusatory piety that relished the suffering to come for some people—some sooner than others—and a self-satisfied assertion of exactly who those people were, people the Lord had cursed. It was right there in the Bible.

They lit the cross, the leader raised his hands and asked us to bow our heads. I felt myself start to do that but held back. A photo snapped a second earlier would have shown me lowering my head, a gesture that would speak for itself, and forever.

And where would *I* be, the one who thought he could *explain*, the one who so easily and smugly set himself apart? The photograph would travel and testify, and it would not do me the courtesy of a summons that allowed me to try to justify myself. And the image would *not* be a lie. I was there. I had believed I could be a witness but not a participant. I had believed I could stand *outside* history and use it for my own entertainment.

I know now that the Klan was not about to become extinct—just the opposite, somehow—and they were certainly no joke.

When I came to this college, the security questionnaire I filled out asked if I had ever been a member of, or attended a meeting of, a long list of organizations. It included the Communist Party, as I recall, and it included the Ku Klux Klan. I answered no to everything. I never gave it another thought.

## *33.*

Those are the only pages of the talk I have. There's a final section, where I mention W. E. B. Du Bois's double consciousness and suggest that something similar might have manifested itself in reverse fashion for me during my time at the college. That was an unfortunate thing for me to say. I wouldn't say it now.

The conference took place at the same time a review of security procedures was ongoing at the college, begun soon after the attacks on the World Trade Center. The ad hoc committee, chaired by Dr. Vikram Patel, noted the inconsistency of my security questionnaire with what I'd said. This was included in the report to the president, who called me in and told me I wouldn't be offered another contract. But I had confessed publicly to attending a Klan meeting and to lying about it, and when I gave that talk, I knew what I was doing.

## *34.*

Donnie and I are watching the Georgia football game. Suzanne steps into the room. I haven't seen her or heard from her in a week.

"Oh, hey," she says to me. "I wasn't really expecting to see you here." She tells Donnie she knocked and tried the bell, but when nobody answered, she walked in.

"Yeah, that doorbell's busted. Charlotte's in the back. She'll be ready in a minute."

Suzanne goes down the hall. Donnie's holding Iris on his lap. She wriggles away from him and approaches the TV and wants "Curious George," her favorite cartoon.

"George, Pa." She runs to Donnie. "*George*, say please?"

They have the show on DVD, and she gets to watch it whenever she wants to, but the football game is on.

Donnie says, "George ain't on now, baby. Only the football game."

"No," she says, "George."

"Not now, Iris, we need to watch this game."

Georgia completes a long pass, Donnie and I shout and startle Iris, her face contorts, and she runs toward the back of the house.

Donnie gets up and heads for the hallway, but comes back. "Looks like Suzanne's got her."

In a few minutes, we hear a door slam. When there's a time-out, Donnie goes to check, and everybody's gone.

When Charlotte gets home, she tells me that Suzanne talked with her about what happened a week ago. "She knows how sick you are, and she does want to spend time with you, but it's hard for her."

## *35.*

Monday morning, Suzanne calls. We talk for a while, and now she's driving us out to see Dwayne Howard's cabin, but we're not even sure we're on the right road. She takes a left, the two-lane drops into a canyon of pine and shadow.

She talks about her friend Michelle, about how close the two had once been. She's quiet for a while, and then she tells me that Michelle took her own life.

"It seems there's an epidemic of suicide," she says. "But I'm sure you know that."

"Well, yes, I do."

"Have you ever been close to anybody who did that?"

"I have."

“But it’s hidden,” she says. “It’s a hidden epidemic. I’ve never seen an obituary that said ‘after a long battle with crippling depression.’ Those notices probably exist, but I’ve never seen one.”

*36.*

The year they were to graduate, Ronaldo and Daliah Viera, students from Trinidad, became the parents of a little girl. Daliah missed the fall quarter but came back in January. I have an image of her sitting in my class, but I can’t see her face clearly. After midnight, three weeks into the quarter, I got a call from the dean. She was with a student who needed to speak to me. It was Ronaldo, who apologized for calling so late and then told me that Daliah had died. I asked him what happened. He said, “Well,”—there was a long pause and I didn’t know if he was still there—“she died.” A scrambling rattle, and then the dean had the phone again. “I think it would be good if you came over first thing in the morning,” she said. “Ronaldo’s not in good shape. He’s got a cousin from Trinidad who lives in Mississippi, and he’s apparently on his way, but there’s nobody in this area. He’s mentioned your name several times, and I think it would be good if you could come. It doesn’t have to be right now, but first thing in the morning. He’s okay for now, I think. Hold on a minute.” I heard a door close. The dean spoke softly. “Daliah took her own life, so…” She gave me directions to the couple’s apartment, where Ronaldo would show me the pipe that had held the rope, and I would listen to the baby’s wind-up swing tick-tocking back and forth in the next room.

*37.*

I wake up in the night, fighting for air, sick with fear and confused, bewildered by sorrow and regret. My teeth grind on their own. A rotting smell, a putrid meat odor, a screw torqued down into the back of my throat, an overflow of the sloshing in my head. I sit up, it rushes to spill out through my eyes, I roll toward the trash bag by the bed and vomit onto the sad evidence of my life's work, and I feel a little better.

*38.*

When Zora Neale Hurston was nine years old, she decided to walk to the horizon. "Now *that's* Zora," Dr. Caruthers said. "That is the essence of the girl and the woman, right there. She never stopped trying. She had her eye on the horizon all her life."

I was sitting in the back seat as Suzanne drove Charlotte and me to a store in Athens. They had persuaded me to come along for the ride. I wouldn't be shopping. We had gone about five miles. Charlotte asked Suzanne if she and her husband had traveled much. They'd visited England and France and Italy, Suzanne told her. They'd been to Mexico and Canada. They loved Montreal. "Donnie and I went to Paris that one time," Charlotte said. I started to feel sick. I asked Suzanne to take me back to the motel, and she did.

I have lived a small life. I was reconciled to that a long time ago. But I'm beginning to realize—and I can already feel myself pushing the realization away, even as it comes to me—

that as small as my life has been, I've been strangely absent from it.

*39.*

We're sitting at the kitchen table. "You know," Charlotte says, "I don't believe I've ever known what David did for a living." Suzanne's face brightens, and when she answers, she's not looking at Charlotte but at me.

"David worked for the National Weather Service in Raleigh. He was a meteorologist."

I said, "That's a joke, right?"

"No it's not, Everett. I married the weatherman."

Charlotte is startled by our laughter, which continues for a moment, and there's a peculiar feeling in my chest, as if a small thing has clicked into place briefly then fallen out, and I feel like I'm sixteen again, helpless in Suzanne's presence. She's so beautiful. All I can do is look at her.

*40.*

Dr. Caruthers didn't finish her biography. There had been a surge of interest in Zora Neale Hurston. Someone else had published a biography, and another was in the works. Dr. Caruthers was glad to see the long overdue attention, and she made use of her research by offering a Special Topics class on the work and life of Zora Neale Hurston.

Somebody told me Dr. Caruthers had once written a novel. "I never even sent it out," she said when I asked her about it. "It's not much of a novel. It does tell a story, but too often the writing feels didactic, and the characters are little essays on legs. That's how I wrote them. Nobody ever talked that way. But that's what it took for me to get it written.

"I wrote it under the spell of *Their Eyes Were Watching God*, which it doesn't resemble in the slightest. A central piece of the story involves a strange coincidence, exactly the sort of thing that prompts people to say if you put such a thing in a novel, no one would believe it. I tried to leave it out but couldn't manage it, I guess, because it really did happen, and it happened to me. That's the sort of temptation a better writer would overcome, but I couldn't. And the ending is sentimental, no doubt about it, but that doesn't bother me at all. It's the right ending."

## *41.*

A month after Dr. Reid's funeral, Mrs. Reid asked Camille and me to come over. She asked me to pick up a cheese pizza. We ate in the kitchen. Mrs. Reid said nothing about what had happened when I visited Dr. Reid at the hospital in Savannah, and I was grateful.

The house was dark. The door to Dr. Reid's study was closed. Camille was already there when I arrived. She'd been helping catalog some of Dr. Reid's papers. Mrs. Reid intended to look closely at every page before she let it go into the archive, and the process was likely to take a long time. Esmeralda would be arriving next week to help out.

Mrs. Reid ate almost none of the pizza and only a few bites of the salad she'd made. She was still in the old clothes she'd worn while she worked. There was a stack of paper on the counter. "That's the manuscript," she said. "They still want it. Wallace Lee never could bring himself to let it go."

"Dr. Reid was always a perfectionist," I said.

"*Perfectionist* is not the word. He was extremely thorough, but he was not after perfection, which he thought was a naive concept. He didn't think anything was perfect, and especially no work of history, which was always fragmentary, and to his way of thinking, always partly fiction."

She gave a real smile for the first time that evening, and her face came alive as she recalled how Dr. Reid had loved to quote Voltaire: "History is tricks we play on the dead."

"All that week in the hospital," she told us, "I knew it was coming, I knew it was close, I felt its presence. But then it was sudden, as if a doorknob had come off in my hand and I was stranded on this side and Wallace Lee was on the other, just like that, nothing to be done about it."

I came across a passage Dr. Reid had marked through, with the delete symbol in the margin. It was about a white woman from Albany, Georgia, in 1926, who had written a letter to the newspaper saying that she would not hesitate to slaughter the entire black race to save one white child.

*42.*

A page of notes on a "sense of presence" during bereavement

> -at its weakest, it is a sense that one is being watched by the deceased; at its strongest it is a full-blown sensory experience—olfactory, auditory, visual, even tactile.

-case studies mostly involve widows who experience the presence of the husband, though the most common experience is of a deceased parent.

-experiences vary in tone and content. Some bereaved not only feel they are being watched as they perform some ordinary task, but also being helped.

-a common element is the insistence that one was fully awake and not dreaming.

*43.*

Even after she retired, Dr. Caruthers would stop by my office to talk. I told her about my visit with Mrs. Reid. I mentioned the deleted passage about the Albany woman.

"It's a vile thing, isn't it? On the other hand," she said, "I have some understanding of that woman. A few years after my son died, I started hearing about people protesting the use of animals for medical research, and I found myself feeling angry, even though it had nothing to do with Odell. Odell ran out into the street. He didn't have an illness that research could have helped. Still, I knew that if he'd *had* such an illness, and if they'd needed to kill all the rats in the world to keep my baby alive, I'd have wanted them to do it. I'm not proud of feeling like that. I'm just being honest about it. I wouldn't have wanted folks talking to me about rats. So in a way, I do understand that white woman. To her, we were like rats."

*44.*

In the fall of 1994 the Department decided it was time for a reunion of majors, to be held on homecoming weekend. We tried to contact everyone, but turnout was not good. Only twenty-three attended, but out of those, several had done well. Carlos Fluellen had gone on to study at Penn State, where he got his doctorate. He was a clinician in Ohio, doing cognitive-behavioral therapy with adolescents. Shirley Willard was a county school superintendent in Alabama. Reginald Rucker had served in the Army as an intelligence officer and retired as a major. He was about to start a job teaching social science and coaching softball at a high school in Chatham County. People said Gold Monkey owned a house in the exclusive Lullwater area of Atlanta, near Emory. There was no reliable word of Latrice Glover, though someone had heard she lived in New York City. Jamal Malik, once Andrew Stubbs, had gone into real estate, then worked for a Georgia congressman, a Republican. He was now with a large firm of lobbyists. I ended up spending most of my time talking with him. He seemed very curious about my life, but that was likely his professional self in operation. I asked him if he knew what became of Yusef Ishmael, his close friend and mentor. I knew he was still on campus when Jamal Malik graduated, and that he had vanished two years later in the middle of fall quarter. Having occupied a spot in the student center for over a decade, Yusef Ishmael was abruptly gone. People wondered if he had finally made his way to Ghana, where he was said to own land. But then somebody told me they thought he had gone home to Macon to be there with his elderly mother when she needed somebody to take care of her. Nobody knew the truth, and neither did Jamal Malik, who spoke about his old friend in a dismissive fashion. I didn't expect to hear that.

Several people were no longer with us, and there was a display of photographs. Tiffany Raiford died eight years before. I knew she'd spent time in the women's prison at Hardwick. Isaac Bell's photo was there.

Somebody said Danielle was a Pentecostal Holiness minister with a church in Sparta. I was able to confirm that. I had heard her on AM radio once as I drove to Augusta. Her voice carried a frightening authority. She was preaching on the words Jesus spoke from the cross.

I listened until I lost the signal, and I turned around and tried to pick it up again but couldn't.

## *45.*

When we were planning the reunion, I wrote to Walt, thinking he might want to visit, even though he'd only spent that one year at the college. He didn't make the reunion, but when he came to Atlanta a year later to present a paper at a conference, I drove up there and we had dinner.

Walt and Lisa have two boys. He teaches at the University of Connecticut, and she owns a consulting business. Apparently, they're very comfortable.

I'd made a reservation for us at an upscale place in Buckhead, but Walt didn't want that. He'd looked forward to barbecue, so I took him to Fat Matt's Rib Shack, where we shared a slab of ribs. He had a beer, and I had an iced tea. Later, when I refilled my glass and he ordered another beer, he said, "I guess you're an iced tea man now."

"I'm not drinking these days, if that's what you mean."

The small place was loud and packed and too hot. There was a line out the door, and the outer door was propped open by people wedged into the vestibule. A couple was sharing our table, and the woman struggled to hold a child of maybe three on her lap and eat her ribs at the same time. The traffic out on Piedmont fumed in place, locked in the normal state of affairs for a late Friday afternoon in Atlanta.

We talked about some of the people we'd both known.

"It occurs to me," he said, "that I've never told you why we left before the funeral."

"Well, I had a good idea. People asked me where you were. I said I didn't know."

"Yeah, it sort of did me in. And being around you didn't help things much, the way you were, you know. I mean, I'm sorry, but…"

"Yeah, I do know, I do. Don't worry about it, Spaceman."

He delivered his explosive laugh, a single loud *Hah*. The woman sitting next to him jumped.

"God," he said. "Spaceman. I'd totally forgotten about that. As I remember it now, I kind of enjoyed being the Spaceman. I don't believe Lisa ever knew people called me that. I don't think I ever told her."

"You should tell her. How's she doing?"

"Oh, she's fine, she's great. She's sort of a star in her world, you know. She sends her greetings."

"What did she think about us doing this? I don't imagine she thought it was a good idea."

"She wasn't wild about it, that's true, but she didn't really object. After we left, you know, she called you a slow-motion suicide. I disagreed. You were clearly doing harm to yourself—anybody could see that—but I didn't think it was intentional, just that you hadn't really grown up yet. I didn't think you were actually trying to kill yourself."

"I wasn't."

I realized that the couple at our table had stopped eating and were holding still, looking down at their plates.

I allowed Walt to think I had quit drinking, but only a few weeks earlier I'd been too drunk to drive home after the party at Camille's house. The reason I didn't have a beer with Walt was that I'd been taking an antibiotic that would have interacted with the alcohol and made me sick. But for some reason I don't really understand and don't want to examine too closely, I continued my abstinence. That was seven years ago, and I haven't had a drink since, except for the day I was diagnosed, when I got dead-drunk and in the end wished I could go ahead and die. It helped for about three hours, and then it made everything much worse.

## *46.*

A cataract sky all day, dirty light through a membrane. A great day to run, cool with a little mist. Claude had put in sixteen miles that morning.

He said, "I believe that's about as far as I can go." He and Arlene were sitting quietly on the sofa. He had his arm around her. I'd never seen him look so tired.

Camille said the library had received a new collection of personal narratives. "Histories of black people in the South, as far back as 1870. Wallace Lee, you'll be familiar with some of this, but some of these are untold stories."

"You know," Walt said, "there are theorists who maintain that the untold story actually doesn't exist, *can't* exist."

“What could that possibly mean?” she asked.

“They say we don’t have a story until it’s *told*, until it’s given a shape. Before that, we do have something, but it’s not a story.”

“Of *course* it’s not.” Arlene’s voice was strange—clotted and low, as if she had a really bad cold. She was staring at the floor, and she looked agitated. She kept fidgeting. Camille moved to sit with her on the sofa and took her hand.

“It might be a question of audience,” Walt said. “Of who *authenticates* the story.”

“Wilma sure is late getting here,” Mrs. Reid said. “I wonder if there’s a problem. If Wilma were here, she’d straighten this out for us.”

Nobody knew where she was.

When Arlene raised her eyes, she was a woman I had never seen. She glared from person to person. She spoke in that low, alien voice at alarming volume.

“Only *God* can tell the story. *You’re not God.*”

She jerked away from Camille, swung her elbow and caught Camille on the arm and lurched up from the couch and walked drunkenly and fast—she was not drunk—down the hall and slammed the door.

Camille started to follow but Claude took her by the wrist and shook his head and drew her back to the sofa.

At the end of this gray day, the sun came out as it was going down, the breeze picked up, and the light flashed silver in the leaves and the grass.

When it was time for us to go, Dr. Oliver played “Clair de Lune” on the piano—a melody that speaks to me even now in some essential way, about what the world is and is not.

As Dr. Oliver played, Arlene came back into the room, walking slowly, holding herself carefully, as if she were a vessel that might spill, a chalice or a wooden cup. She took her place beside Claude and laid her head on his shoulder.

*47.*

Claude did have faith, but his faith told him that the universe is indifferent to us.

"If there is any caring to be done," he once said to me, "we'll have to do it ourselves, and I can't think of anything more important for us to understand than that."

*48.*

Donnie and Charlotte are driving to Nashville right this minute. I'm at their house. Elizabeth has had an altercation with her husband. They tried to convince her to come home, but she won't. They'll be back late tomorrow, and they intend to bring Elizabeth with them, though she might not know that. Suzanne is on her way here now to keep Iris. She had an early appointment in Atlanta. Donnie talked to her right before they left, which was a little before noon.

"She was already in Snellville. She'll be here in about half an hour. The baby will sleep till around two o'clock."

Charlotte has left instructions for everything. I'm amazed at what she did in such a short time. She laid out clothes and planned every meal and every snack and arranged the food in discrete meal and snack units and put them in the refrigerator. They wanted to take the baby with them, but Elizabeth wouldn't have it. She didn't want the child brought back into that situation.

I meant to ask Donnie if he still had his pistol in the car, but I forgot.

*49.*

It was in 1992, while at a conference in Savannah, that Dr. Reid had a stroke. He died five days later in a hospital there. I drove up two days after the stroke.

At his room, I knocked and heard someone tell me to come in. I cracked the door and saw Mrs. Reid and her daughter, Esmeralda. There was a toxic odor, like plastic burning.

When I stepped inside, Dr. Reid sat up in bed, and what I saw in half his face was raw hate. He jabbed at me with his finger and kept jabbing, and he spoke words that sounded like "I *know* you," and he kept on saying that.

I almost ran from the room, and I was a few steps down the hall when a loud squawk came over the intercom, a garbled blurt that ended with a harsh pop, as if something had snapped in half.

*50.*

My grandmother and I were on Highway 78. We had just passed Stone Mountain, and we were not far from Emory hospital when she told me the story of how my grandfather had come to be at Moore's Ford.

He'd been walking down Snow's Mill Road when an acquaintance, a man she didn't name, drove by and stopped and offered him a ride. He got in the car, then learned that the man had heard there was trouble out that way, and he was headed toward it.

"Arlo was there by accident. But then he stood there and watched it happen. He'd wake up at night hearing the screams those women made when the men dragged them out of the car. He prayed for forgiveness every day of his life, but I don't think he ever felt it. Maybe he didn't ask for it in the right way. The truth is, he was scared to death. We both were."

She made me promise, on the soul of my mother, never to say a word about what she'd told me.

## *51.*

Suzanne ought to be here by now. She doesn't answer her cell phone. I check on Iris and sit beside her and listen to her breathe for a while, then ease my way out of the room and close the door. Static washes through the TV room from the baby monitor. The TV is turned on but muted. I tune it to the weather channel, and I can see that Donnie and Charlotte are driving into trouble. The radar shows a line of storms heavy with red, tilting to the right, headed east and moving fast. It looks like the tail of that line will sweep across us before too long. We will soon be under a severe thunderstorm watch. Suzanne doesn't answer her phone. I leave a message saying I hope she'll be here soon.

## *52.*

Dr. Oliver had played "Clair de Lune." The day was done. As we headed out the door, Claude said he and Arlene would be driving to St. Simons in the morning, where they planned to stay for a couple of days.

That night they swallowed enough pills and drank enough vodka and lay down in their upstairs bedroom dressed for sleep. They were found curled together, a single shape, his arm around her, his face in her hair, a Bible in her arms, the bed turned to the east.

The cancer had gone to her brain, and Arlene had begun to lose herself—she had lost herself—in ways she refused to allow. She could not abide the stranger she had become, and she wanted to kill her, and she did. They had no children and no close kin. They left a note addressed to Mabel and Wallace Lee Reid and Wilma Caruthers.

Some people aimed their hurt anger at Arlene for letting Claude go with her, as though Claude could have been told what to do. Stay, boy. And who could have held him back? That last morning, he had run sixteen miles.

It was no surprise that Claude lay down with Arlene and held her close in their last hour. It was no surprise that he would not let Arlene go into the dark alone.

"Hell no," I can hear him say. "*Hell* no."

*53.*

REMEMBER

*for Arlene and Claude*

Clouds scud up from the south, white clouds,
and now there is a body with a head,

but I turn away to put this down
on a note card, and when I look at the sky

again, into the blue no one can capture,
there is no creature in the heavens anymore.

Maybe an odd mouth, a wisp of white hair,
but the liquid history of the clouds

leads me to believe we are the weather,
we are the dust and the rain of yesterday,

and once upon a time, once upon our time,
yesterday, the dust swirled up,

and the dust hung in the air a little while,
and the rain came down and rose again

and made a lens in the air that held it,
and we beheld the world. We remember you,

we remember who you were.

*54.*

At 1:30 Iris is awake. The instructions say it's time to feed her. I assemble the meal Charlotte has prepared. I put Iris in the high chair, strap her in and snap the tray in place. I manage to force it into position wrongly, so that it sits at an angle, and I have to wrestle it off and try again. Iris appears unconcerned through all this—I've given her a few small cubes of cheese—but now, after I've fixed the tray and she has finished the cheese, her mouth turns down. There's alarm in her eyes, and I don't know what has happened. I pick up a giraffe and dance it across the tray and she reaches out for it, still appearing dismayed but not in tears. She eats bits of ham and grape and banana, and I feed her spoonfuls of applesauce. Charlotte has halved the grapes, but I'm not sure the bites are small enough, so I halve them again. Iris likes the bananas best. When she finishes, I wash the smushed bananas off her hands and face. After lunch I change her, paying close attention to Charlotte's instructions—left for me, just in case—about how to properly clean her. I finally get her dressed and stand her up and she runs into the TV room, and I call Suzanne. No answer.

## *55.*

The last night of Dr. Calder's conference, on a pleasant evening in late April, he hosted a reception at his home, an expansive, comfortable house that opened onto a large garden patio.

I took a seat at a table occupied by two other conference participants—Dr. Joyce Marion, an African-American woman probably in her mid-thirties who taught history at Lincoln University, and a biology professor from Cameroon, a Dr. Afana, who taught at Morehouse and seemed to be about my age. I remembered them from the program and from their presentations.

As I sat down, I said to Dr. Marion, "Do you mind?"

"Of course not."

"But I haven't formally introduced myself," I said. "I'm Everett Moon. I teach psychology here at the college."

"Oh, I know. I'm Joyce Marion. I heard your talk this afternoon. It made quite an impression on me."

I said thanks.

Dr. Afana stood and shook my hand and excused himself to speak to someone.

"No," Dr. Marion said, "you shouldn't thank me, and perhaps I should keep my thoughts to myself—I don't mean to be unkind—but you see, I was not impressed in a *favorable* way. Your talk was familiar and troubling. I found myself feeling angry and sad at the same time. The Germans probably have a word for it."

"I'm sorry," I said. "Was it the thing about the Klan?"

"Oh no." She gave me a grim smile. "No, that was no surprise at all, not in the least. No. Take a good look at your talk. This is a conference on institutions that have been crucial in the struggle and survival of African-Americans, and what you gave us was yet another version of the very familiar so-called redemption narrative of a white person. This is the kind of thing we see all the time in novels and memoirs. Having had some experience with black people, the white author finds himself or herself transformed and enlightened and living with a sense of having acquired some strange new racial credential, self-assigned though it may be. Rarely does this new knowledge cost very much, and rarely does the story acknowledge the baffling complications of *every* human story. It usually contains considerable melodrama, almost always with exotic overtones."

A man walking past as she said this turned back and moved toward the table. "All right if I sit here?"

Dr. Marion nodded. She turned her attention back to me. "But that's it. No need to belabor the point. We can leave it there."

The man was Frederick Ames, a political scientist from Prairie View. "I apologize for butting in," he said to Dr. Marion, "but I overheard some of your conversation and felt compelled to say that I had a similar reaction."

He spoke to me then with a tone of accusation I didn't expect. "I've seen *your* kind before. You show up and you're so humbly white, and so *proud* of your humility, and you want to be *praised* for it. And then you'll have some kind of conversion experience because we have treated you with common decency. Your expectations have been overthrown, and we should be pleased and feel *validated* by you. It's a real part of the problem, white folks like you who think they've *crossed over* somehow, white folks who want to sidle up next to us and get cozy because of some kind of new status you assume you've earned. Of course, *your* case involves an odd condescension from below, since you're so comfortable down there.

"And your story is predicated—this is not your fault, though; this is a structural problem—on the assumption that truth is measured by how a white person sees it, that the opinion of a white person is by default the source of our authentication."

I could see no way to disagree with what he'd said, but neither could I see a way to tell him that without engaging in some form of white authentication. I stayed quiet.

"But what I mainly see is this," he said. "One more white man with a black fetish, gratifying himself out in the open and feeling fine."

"That's a bit harsh," Dr. Marion said, "don't you think? I mean, I'm with you on most of what you've said, but.... But look, let me say this to *you*, Dr. Ames. When you say that we have treated Professor Moon with common decency, well, no. That's not true. *We* didn't. You and I were not part of what happened. We just met him. *They*, the people at this college, treated him with common decency."

"Yes, but you know what I mean."

"I do know what you mean, and I don't agree with it. A race takes no actions. Individuals take actions, singly or together. Now, individuals can band together and declare that they are acting *as* a race. We've certainly seen enough of that in this country. But that's not what has happened here."

I caught myself looking for Dr. Caruthers, who had passed away only weeks earlier. I kept expecting to see her. I missed her.

"Although," Dr. Marion said to me, "I *will* have to point out—and this is what I was about to say when I was interrupted—what I found most problematic was the way you ended your talk, trying to incorporate into your own life Du Bois's concept of double consciousness. That was absolutely appalling to me.

"Yes, I can see that you might have felt a glimmer of something similar when you needed to gauge how you were seen through the eyes of your black superiors, but listen, even to mention that in the same breath with the words of W. E. B. Du Bois, given the unbearable weight of the tragic history his words carried, is evidence of a kind of spiritual *gall*. It displays a stunning lack of understanding."

Dr. Calder and his wife emerged from the house and without a word to Dr. Marion or to me, Dr. Ames left us to join them. He took the president's hand in both of his and praised the conference in animated fashion.

"He's a delight, isn't he?" Dr. Marion said, and she laughed. "Since I've gone this far," she said, "there's one other concern I want to raise with you. This is a matter of lesser importance, and it's something that you may not even be aware of, but that you *need* to be aware of, which is this: There's a certain recognizable tone and cadence and inflection in the way you speak and carry yourself. This is not all that unusual, of course, given your long time here. People acquire mannerisms of all kinds from those around them. It's a kind of protective mimicry. Even so, I have to say that in your case, for whatever reason, it's disturbing to witness. Sometimes I detect a hint of performance, and I'm sure you don't want that. I certainly hope not. I'm not saying it's blackface, you understand, but it's inclined that way. Let's just leave it at that."

She said, "If you think I've been rude, I hope you'll forgive me. That was not my intention. I just found it necessary to say something to you about your grasp of where you are and where you've been. I was curious to know if you're aware of certain things. And so, well, now I've said it, I've said what I had to say. You know what, though? I *would* like to hear about some of the students you've had during your time here. Something about who they've been and what they have become, what they've accomplished."

I did have stories to tell her, and I told a few of them.

Zora Neale Hurston claimed certain white people as genuine friends. She also felt insulted "when a certain type of white person hastens to effuse to me how noble they are to grant me their presence."

*56.*

When Dr. Reid showed me the Moore's Ford articles, I told him how I learned about the lynching but I said nothing about my grandfather. I've never even told Donnie. If I spoke out now, the entire moral weight of the atrocity would be on Arlo Moon, and only Arlo Moon. The right thing to do would be to tell the truth, but I don't plan to do that.

So there it is.

*57.*

From *Bootleg Yesterday*
Camille Williams

HERITAGE

How do, Mr. Crow? How do?
I *do* know yo boy Joe.

He sho do look like you,
Mr. Crow. He *sho* do.

*58.*

The lights go out, the TV dies, Iris looks up, something beeps once, I step onto the back porch, the wind hits hard enough to slap the dogwood sideways and hold it there. Sirens. Iris is running and crying, I have her in my arms, the walls shake and warp, the air groans, I make it to the basement door, onto the stairs, my knee buckles, and we're falling.

When their son died of whooping cough at age two, William James and his wife sat with a medium, hoping for a word from their lost child. The universe itself, James believed, might be endowed with consciousness, even with love.

"To anyone who has ever looked on the face of a dead child or parent," he wrote, "the mere fact that matter could have taken for a time that precious form, ought to make matter sacred for ever after.... That beloved incarnation was among matter's possibilities."

And if matter, having become the beloved, is sacred forever, time must be sacred too—that element in which matter's possibilities play out. Year by year, day by day, hour by hour, holy second holy second holy second.

*59.*

Yesterday. Was it yesterday? Donnie was here. Suzanne was here. They said Iris was all right, not even a scratch, Donnie said. She was at home with Charlotte and Elizabeth.

"You hit your head. You been in and out the last couple of days. Out, mostly. They say you can come home with us tomorrow or the day after."

Suzanne's phone died right after she talked to Donnie. She didn't have a charger in the car. She was in Snellville when the traffic backed up and came to a dead stop and stayed that way for half an hour. She never did find out why. And before she got to Loganville, it backed up again because of a wreck. She got to the house just as the storm hit.

## 60.

The funeral overflowed Christ Chapel AME, a white-frame church in the middle of peach fields, half a mile out Carver Drive. One o'clock on a Thursday. People stood along the walls. I looked for Lisa and Walt but didn't see them. The service was short. There was the invocation, a reading of scripture, a hymn and a solo. Then Dr. Reid spoke briefly about Claude, Dr. Caruthers spoke about Arlene, and she was followed by the minister. Another hymn, a prayer, and that was it.

Dr. Reid had to smile. "You don't need me to tell you who Claude Jackson was—a man of great talent and wit and energy and generosity. But I do want to tell you something about him that you may not know. You may not be aware that Claude was a man of means. He was not wealthy by the wider world's standards, but he had money, and quite a bit of money, the result of an inheritance from an aunt. Claude and Arlene never lived as if they had any money. He drove that old pickup and she drove her Galaxy, but they could have both been driving a Mercedes. Claude was a close observer of the young people at the college, and when he came across someone or heard of someone who especially needed or deserved his help, he gave it to them. He did this anonymously, through the college administration—full scholarships as well as other assistance if it was needed, help that went beyond what any scholarship would do. Medical bills, lawyers' bills, even assistance to families in danger of losing their homes. Claude wanted none of this to be known. Arlene was of the same mind. What large and generous hearts they had. They have left everything to the college. Their good work will continue.

"Now, I feel a need to say this too: I stand before you today in this church where Arlene worshipped, but where I am not a member and where Claude was not a member. Claude was true to his convictions, and he did not find it in his heart to follow the Christian faith. Some of you will feel it necessary to lament the state of Claude's soul. If you must do that, well, I suppose you must. But the scripture says judge not. It says by their works ye shall know them. It says inasmuch as ye have done it unto one of the least of these, ye have done it unto me. It says these three abide: faith, hope, and love, but the greatest of these is love. Claude Jackson was not a man of faith, and in the end he was not a man of hope, but who will dare to say that he was not a man of love?"

Dr. Caruthers ascended to the pulpit and stood for a moment with her head bowed before she spoke. "Giving glory to God this afternoon, giving praise in the name of his holy son, Jesus. Let the church say amen." The church said amen. "Our sister Arlene was ill for much longer than most people know. She and Claude had wanted their own children, but her health did not allow it. So they turned to the fullness of their lives together, and to the other lives that they wished to bring close. They knew their time was short, and they spent it the way they desired to. You heard what Wallace Lee said. They had money. They could have been living in Paris, and they had *been* to Paris, they'd been all over, but there was no house in Paris exactly like the one they had created. That was their house, and there was no house like that anywhere but here.

"And there was never a friend to me like Arlene Jackson. Before I came to this college, I lost my son in an accident and went out of my mind and stayed out of my mind, although almost no one could see it. Arlene saw it. When I started to work here, she had been on this campus for only a short while. We were both appointed to serve on an ad hoc committee—I don't even remember what it was for—and we found ourselves together in that old conference room in Miller Hall, listening to the chairman and one other person pontificate and bloviate and puff themselves up week after week. The rest of the committee was willing to focus and do the job, but because of these two, it was an especially toxic waste of time. I always sat in the last chair at the far end of the table, and Arlene sat across from me. There came a day when one of those personalities flared up again and weighed in with his one question everyone knew was coming, after which, as we all knew he would, he veered off into some personal story that showed him in a flattering light. Somewhere in his routine, his signature verbal tic, 'if I do say so myself' was bound to appear.

"That afternoon when he got around to saying so himself, Arlene raised her head and looked straight at me, her eyes deadpan but asking for help, and a little yip of a laugh erupted from my throat, and everybody looked my way, and I coughed unconvincingly. I felt so foolish. As we left the conference room, she touched me on the elbow, and we held back and let the others go on, and when we were alone, we laughed until we had to sit down.

"I laughed that day until I was empty and full all at once, and then I began to sob and it all poured out of me, I choked and shook, and Arlene put her arms around me. She took part of my grief into herself. I felt it. I felt something *leave* me, as if an ill spirit had been drawn out. Arlene Jackson was an instrument of *grace* in my life, and from that day until the day she died, she was my sister. In time, she led me to see that I had indeed been blessed. I had known the brief embrace of a child who loved me. In the name of our Lord and Savior Jesus Christ, let us *raise up* Arlene and Claude Jackson today. Let us say amen to the lives they lived among us. Let us say amen to this good woman and to this good man. May the Lord bless them and keep them until we meet again."

Rev. Leander McGhee told us how, one Sunday last year, he had led the church in singing "Precious Lord," and after he'd sat down, as the deacons went along the aisles with the collection plates, as the piano kept playing, he had continued to be under the spell of the hymn, whistling it softly, unaware it was being picked up by his lapel mic. Arlene found him afterwards and told him that everyone had heard him whistling. He was embarrassed, but she made sure that he knew she had sought him out to tell him how beautiful it had been, and how much it had moved her and others too. Rev. McGhee led us in singing that same hymn, and after he had raised his hands and asked us to bow our heads and close our eyes, as we stood there awaiting the benediction, the piano continued. He said, "I know Arlene is listening," and he whistled a single verse of "Precious Lord." It was thrilling to the bone, ghostly and true. I have never heard anything like it.

*61.*

*(sometimes i feel like i'm almost going)*
*to Chicago. baby you want to go?*
from *American Sonnets*
—Wanda Coleman

A wakeful dream of Chicago, where I've never been. Thousands of strangers, oblivious to who I am, going past me, out on the streets this minute, all of it happening without me, but now I'm there, I'm being carried along on a river of lives made of ecstasy and sorrow and tenderness and tragedy and desire and suffering and hard laughter and boredom and wisdom and yearning and regret and confusion and nostalgia and nausea and satisfaction and despair and wonder and abandon and envy and fascination and hope and rage and breakdown and curiosity and worship and dancing together and surrender and hurt and release and heartbreak and love song and being lost and drifting away and salvation and coming home to the beloved and drifting away, and on and on and on, all these lives, each one infinitely deep and beyond me, going on beyond me—right now in Chicago, out on the streets of Chicago, where I have never been—but taking me with them, and I'm washed along on this river of strangers that bears me away till I'm gone, a long way from home. I want to go.

*62.*

I mostly stay in bed, but when I'm up to it, I sit on the sofa and watch *Curious George* with Iris. If I can do that, it's the best part of my day. At times I feel like the Man with the Yellow Hat. I wish I could *be* the Man with the Yellow Hat.

## *63.*

Suzanne has sold her mother's house. She has packed up everything, movers are set to haul it all back to Raleigh, and she's leaving tomorrow. Thomas and Marie will be meeting her at home. There's an excitement about her now that I haven't seen before.

It's a six-hour drive. She needs to be there by one o'clock, and she's leaving before dawn. She'd planned to stay in a motel, but Charlotte wouldn't hear of it and insisted Suzanne have dinner here and sleep in one of the guest rooms.

Charlotte has made a few of her daughter's favorites—chicken pot pie, fried okra and mashed potatoes and a chocolate cake. I can eat only a few bites of the mashed potatoes.

Elizabeth wants to know about the storm. Donnie says the tornado took down trees along McDaniel Street.

"Just so you know," Suzanne tells us, "it was not actually a tornado but a downdraft that did the damage—very much like a tornado, but different."

She smiles at me, and I feel it again, that little click in my chest. She's laughing and I'm laughing, and I'm astonished that we are here at all, as opposed to being nowhere.

The fact of the world seems miraculous, and the existence of everything in time and the way we are sailing through the universe together—this minute, at this table, in this house, on this planet.

I look at my brother and his family, I look at Suzanne, I take a drink of the sweet, iced tea and when it hits my throat—in that moment, before it's gone—it holds all the goodness of life.

*64.*

We move into the TV room and sit around watching Iris play.

"For just a few minutes," Elizabeth says. "It's bedtime."

"No." Iris slings a giraffe at the barn.

"All right now, none of that, or we'll have to go to bed right this minute."

She runs toward the TV and points at it.

"No, it's too late for that," Elizabeth says, and she holds out her arms. "Come here and I'll read you a story."

Iris runs to the sofa and jumps into her mother's arms. Elizabeth shuffles the books on the end table, looking for the right one, but before she has found it, Iris crawls across the sofa and onto my lap. She lays her head against my chest.

"That's a tired baby," Charlotte says.

Elizabeth says, "Yes, she is. Let's tell everybody good night, pumpkin. Tell Uncle Everett good night."

Iris squirms upward until the top of her head is pressed against my cheek. The smell of baby hair is faintly bread-like and sweet. Elizabeth reaches down to lift her, and when Iris throws her arm around my neck and clings to me, I am stunned to realize that I have never felt this before, a child holding me tight and not wanting to let go, as though she loved me. I have never had this feeling before, not once in my life. Never. But I have had it now.

## *65.*

And this dream is being dreamed by someone else, but I'm awake inside it now, and I ease through each room in the house and stand beside the others, one by one, and watch them sleep. They must be dreaming too. But I'm awake. I know I am. I'm with Suzanne, out on the highway, driving under stars that have turned the night sky blue, the tires are crackling on the road, and we are closer to the horizon than we have ever been, so close to the jagged edge of heaven and earth, we are nearly able to touch it.

We cross the graveyard. She takes my hand, and we stand here and wait. And this is where we are when the old illusion comes in and the sun seems to rise, though we're falling—I can feel it now, we are falling, all of us, the living and the dead—toward the eastern sky.

## *Author's Note*

This is a work of fiction, revised for many years to locate a spot from which to tell the story. The novel draws on certain aspects of the author's life, but it is a work of the imagination. I grew up in Monroe, Georgia, which is at the heart of the story, where it begins and ends. Like the narrator Everett Moon, I went to teach at an HBCU in 1974 at the age of 26. I taught psychology at Fort Valley State University for 30 years, but I am not Everett Moon, and the unnamed South Georgia college in this story is not Fort Valley State, yet the novel is true to a time and place I witnessed.

## *Notes*

I have identified some sources within the text, and I have quoted from sources, assuming the right to do so either because the source is in the public domain or because I am able to do so under the principle of fair use. When I have drawn from identified sources but did not use quotes, I have tried to paraphrase in appropriate fashion. I do not believe I have drawn on source material without properly crediting and paraphrasing such material. If I have inadvertently done so, I will acknowledge that and will make the necessary corrections.

p. 4: "Strange-face-in-the mirror illusion," Caputo, Giovanni B., *Perception*, 2010, **39**, 1007-1008

p. 6: These are fragments of Heidegger taken from William Barrett's *Irrational Man*.

p. 17: In what is perhaps a unique case, Fort Valley State College was sued by local white citizens. See Bellamy, Donnie D. "Whites Sue for Desegregation in Georgia: The Fort Valley State College Case" *The Journal of Negro History* 1979, vol 64 (4), and Hanks, L.J. 1990. *The Struggle for Black Political Empowerment in Three Georgia Counties.* Anna Holloway's *Looking for Jazz* is an excellent memoir about teaching at Fort Valley State from 1969 to 1972.

p. 66: The material on Zora Neale Hurston was taken from many sources, but the primary source was *Wrapped in Rainbows*, a biography by my late friend Valerie Boyd.

p. 86: From *In the Matter of Color* by Judge Leon Higginbotham, Jr. (1978).

p. 91: Anyone who knows Johnny Morris of Macon, Georgia, will see him in the character of Isaac Bell—in the man's courage and resilience, his inquisitive spirit, the depth of his humor, and his life of faith. We are friends to this day, both of us still in Macon.

p. 119: The character of Aisha grew out of a reading Nikki Giovanni gave at Fort Valley State, in which she used the phrase "the Monroe four." At the time, I did not know what she meant. Laura Wexler's *Fire in a Canebrake* addresses the events at Moore's Ford.

p. 126: The character of L.R. Sterling grew out of a visit by Stokely Carmichael to Fort Valley State, but the talk is modeled on his address at Morgan State University. I drew on that speech and anchored the section around certain points he made there. I have tried to avoid using his exact words, and although a few terms are his, almost all the language in the section is mine, framed by the themes he presented. I worked hard to capture the tone and content of his talk.

p. 132: Fragmentary notes from *The Denial of Death* by Ernest Becker. Some exact language is used, under the assumption that it meets the criteria for fair use.
p. 147: See *Forever Today* by Deborah Wearing (2006)

*****

—The material on William James was taken from many sources

—In 1974 I completed a Ph.D. in biopsychology at the University of Georgia. My major professor, Roger K.Thomas—a prolific researcher and writer in several areas of inquiry, and possessing the sharpest eye of any editor I have encountered—is a close friend to this day and someone to whom I am deeply indebted.